L

'Probably the greatest Scottish novel of the century . . . it marked the beginning of a new era in Scottish writing.' *Observer*

'This extraordinary masterpiece . . . is profoundly perceptive about the ways in which our society is destroying itself. Yet it manages to be funny and is written in a beautifully lucid prose.' *Times Literary Supplement*

'At times exuberant, at times despairing, always vivid voice . . . Curious and informed, angry and rational . . . not afraid of fun or of confessing its vanities or of having Big Ideas.' Janice Galloway, *Sunday Times*

'*Lanark* is one of the seminal works of Scottish literature, a book credited with kick-starting Scotland's literary renaissance of the past two decades.' *Sunday Times*

'Fluent, imaginative, part vision, part realism, even in its organisation it declares itself to be written by the author's rules and no one else's . . . the writing is easy and elegant and never uninteresting.' *Guardian*

'Gray is a master at rummaging in the dustbins of the mind . . . Important and compelling' *Daily Telegraph*

'The most remarkable first novel I've read for years . . . It's unfair that any man, even from Dennistoun, should be so gifted . . . [*Lanark*] is allegorical, factual, political, cannibal (and very much so) . . . this is a book which will be remembered.' *Evening Times*

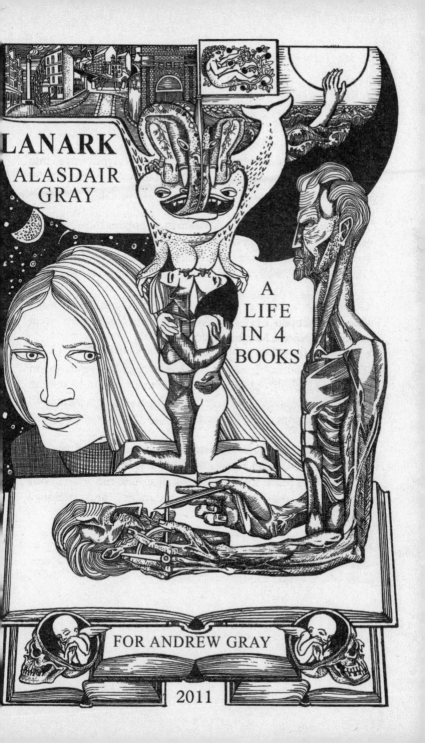

LANARK
ALASDAIR GRAY

A
LIFE
IN 4
BOOKS

FOR ANDREW GRAY

2011

First published in Great Britain in 1981 by
Canongate Publishing Ltd, and republished in 2001
by Canongate Books Ltd, 14 High Street, Edinburgh EH1 1TE

www.meetatthegate.com

Portions of this book originally appeared in *Scottish International Review*,
Glasgow University Magazine and *Works Magazine*

British Library Cataloguing-in-Publication Data
A catalogue record for this book is available on
request from the British Library

ISBN 978 0 85786 008 8

Printed and bound in Great Britain by Clays, St Ives plc

Lanark was originally published in four volumes, in the following order: Book Three, Book One, Book Two and Book Four. What you hold in your hands is Volume Two, Book One, which begins at Chapter Twelve (and on page 121) with the story of the young Duncan Thaw, growing up in post-war Glasgow.

CHAPTER 12. The War Begins

Duncan Thaw drew a blue line along the top of a sheet of paper and a brown line along the bottom. He drew a giant with a captured princess running along the brown line, and since he couldn't draw the princess lovely enough he showed the giant holding a sack. The princess was in the sack. His father looked over his shoulder and said, "What's that you're drawing?"

Thaw said uneasily, "A miller running to the mill with a bag of corn."

"What's the blue line supposed to be?"

"The sky."

"Do you mean the horizon?"

Thaw stared dumbly at his picture.

"The horizon is the line where the sky and land seem to touch. Is it the horizon?"

"It's the sky."

"But the sky isnae a straight line, Duncan!"

"It would be if you saw it sideways."

Mr. Thaw got a golf ball and a table lamp and explained that the earth was like the ball and the sun like the lamp. Thaw was bored and puzzled. He said, "Do people fall off the sides?"

"No. They're kept on by gravity."

"What's ga . . . gavty?"

"*Grrrrr*avity is what keeps us on the earth. Without it we would fly up into the air."

"And then we would reach the sky?"

"No. No. The sky is just the space above our heads. Without gravity we would fly up into it forever."

"But wouldn't we come to a . . . a thing on the other side?"

"There *is* no other side, Duncan. None at all."

Thaw leaned over his drawing and drew a blue crayon along the line of the sky, pressing hard. He dreamed that night of flying up through empty air till he reached a flat blue cardboard sky. He rested against it like a balloon against a ceiling until worried by the thought of what was on the other side; then he broke a hole and rose through more empty air till he grew afraid of floating forever. Then he came to another cardboard sky and rested there till worried by the thought of the other side. And so on.

Thaw lived in the middle storey of a corporation tenement that was red sandstone in front and brick behind. The tenement backs enclosed a grassy area divided into greens by spiked railings, and each green had a midden. Gangs of midden-rakers from Blackhill crossed the canal to steal from the middens. He was told that Blackhill people were Catholics with beasts in their hair. One day two men came to the back greens with a machine that squirted blue flame and clouds of sparks. They cut the spikes from the railings with the flame, put them in a bag and took them away to use in the war. Mrs. Gilchrist downstairs said angrily, "Now even the youngest of these Blackhill kids will be able to rake our middens." Other workmen build air-raid shelters in the back greens and a very big one in the school playground, and if Thaw heard the air-raid warning on the way to school he must run to the nearest shelter. Going up to school by the steep back lane one morning he heard the siren wailing in the blue sky. He was almost at school but turned and ran home to where his mother waited in the back-green shelter with the neighbours. At night dark green blinds were pulled down over the windows. Then Mr. Thaw put on an armband and steel hat and went into the street to search for houses showing illegal chinks of light.

Someone told Mrs. Thaw that the former tenants of her flat had killed themselves by putting their heads in the oven and turning the gas on. She wrote at once to the corporation asking that her gas cooker be changed for an electric one, but as Mr. Thaw would still need food when he returned from work she baked him a shepherd's pie, but with her lips more tightly pursed than usual.

Her son always refused shepherd's pie or any other food whose appearance disgusted him: spongy white tripe, soft penis-like sausages, stuffed sheep's hearts with their valves and little arteries. When one of these came before him he poked it uncertainly with his fork and said, "I don't want it."

"Why not?"

"It looks queer."

"But you havnae tasted it! Taste just a wee bit. For my sake."

"No."

"Children in China are starving for food like that."

"Send it to them."

After more discussion his mother would say in a high-pitched voice, "You'll sit at this table till you eat every bit" or "Just you wait till I tell your father about this, my dear." Then he would put a piece of food in his mouth, gulp without tasting and vomit it back onto the plate. After that he would be shut in the back bedroom. Sometimes his mother came to the door and said, "Will you not eat just a wee bit of it? For my sake?" then Thaw, feeling cruel, shouted "No!" and went to the window and looked down into the back green. He would see friends playing there, or the midden-rakers, or neighbours hanging out washing, and feel so lonely and magnificent that he considered opening the window and jumping out. It was a bitter glee to imagine his corpse thudding to the ground among them. At last, with terror, he would hear his father coming *clomp-clomp* upstairs, carrying his bicycle. Usually Thaw ran to meet him. Now he heard his mother open the door, the mutter of voices in conspiracy, then footsteps coming to the bedroom and his mother whispering, "Don't hurt him too much."

Mr. Thaw would enter with a grim look and say, "Duncan! You've behaved badly to your mother again. She goes to the bother and expense of making a good dinner and ye won't eat it. Aren't ye ashamed of yourself?"

Thaw would hang his head.

"I want you to apologize to her."

"Don't know what 'polgize means."

"Tell her you're sorry and you'll eat what you're given."

Then Thaw would snarl "No, I won't!" and be thrashed.

During the thrashing he screamed a lot and afterward stamped, yelled, tore his hair and banged his head against the wall until his parents grew frightened and Mr. Thaw shouted, "Stop that or I'll draw my hand off yer jaw!"

Then Thaw beat his own face with his fists, screaming, "Like this like this like *this?*"

It was hard to silence him without undoing the justice of the punishment. On the advice of a neighbour they one day undressed the furiously kicking boy, filled a bath with cold water

and plunged him in. The sudden chilling scald destroyed all
his protest, and this treatment was used on later occasions with
equal success. Shivering slightly he would be dried with soft
towels before the living-room fire, then put to bed with his
doll. Before sleep came he lay stunned and emotionless while
his mother tucked him in. Sometimes he considered withhold-
ing the goodnight kiss but could never quite manage it.

When he had been punished for not eating a particular
food he was not given that food again but a boiled egg instead.
Yet after hearing how the former tenants had misused their
oven he looked very thoughtfully at the shepherd's pie when
it was brought to table that evening. At length he pointed
and said, "Can I have some?"
Mrs. Thaw looked at her husband then took her spoon and
plonked a dollop onto Thaw's plate. He stared at the mushy
potato with particles of carrot, cabbage and mince in it and
wondered if brains really looked like that. Fearfully he put
some in his mouth and churned it with his tongue. It tasted
good so he ate what was on the plate and asked for more.
When the meal was over his mother said, "There. You like
it. Aren't ye ashamed of kicking up all that din about nothing?"
"Can I go down to the back green?"
"All right, but come when I call you, it's getting late."
He hurried through the lobby, banged the front door behind
him and ran downstairs, the weight of food in his stomach
making him feel excited and powerful. In the warm evening
sunlight he put his brow to the grass and somersaulted down
a green slope till he fell flat from dizziness and lay with the
tenements and blue sky spinning and tilting round and round
his head. He keeked between the stems of sorrel and daisies
at the midden, a three-sided brick shed where bins were kept.
The sound of voices came indistinctly through the grass blades
to his ears, and the scratchings of a steel-tipped boot on an
iron railing, and the rumble of a bin being shifted. He sat
up.

Two boys slightly older than himself were bent over the
bins and throwing out worn clothes, empty bottles, some pram
wheels and a doormat, while a big boy of ten or eleven put
them in a sack. One of the smaller boys found a hat with a
bird's wing on it. Mimicking the strut of a proud woman he
put it on and said, "Look at me, Boab, am I no' the big cheese?

The older boy said, "Stop that. You'll get the auld wife after us."

He dumped the sack over the railings into the next green and the three of them climbed over to it. Thaw followed by squeezing between the railings then lay down again on the grass. He heard them whisper together and the big boy said, "Never mind about him."

He realized he was frightening them and followed more boldly into the next green, though keeping a distance. He was slightly appalled when the big boy turned and said, "What d'ye want, ye wee bugger?"

Thaw said, "I'm coming with you."

His scalp tightened, his heart knocked on his ribs but this boy had never eaten what he had eaten. The boy with the hat said, "Thump him, Boab!"

Boab said, "Why d'ye want tae come with us?"

"Because."

"Because of what?"

"Nothing. Just because."

"Ye'll have tae carry things if ye come with us. Will ye collect the books?"

"Aye."

"All right then."

After this all magazines and comic papers were left to Thaw, who soon learned which were worth picking from the garbage. They visited every back green in the block, leaving some refuse scattered across each, and were chased from the last by a woman who followed them through her close shouting breathless promises to call the police.

A girl of twelve waited in the street outside holding the handle of a pram with three wheels. She pointed at Thaw and said, "Where did ye pick that up?"

Boab said, "Never mind him," and loaded his sack onto the pram which bulged with rubbish already. The two wee boys harnessed themselves to it with strings tied to the front axle, then with Boab and the girl pushing and Thaw running alongside they went quickly down the street. They passed semi-detached villas with privet hedges, a small power station humming behind aspen trees, allotments with beds of lettuce like green roses and glasshouses glittering in the late sunshine. They went through a gate in a rusty fence and climbed a blue cinder path through a jungle of nettles. The air was thick with vegetable stink, the wee boys groaned with the effort of pulling, a low thundering vibrated the ground under them and at the top they reached the brink of a deep ravine. One end was shut by double doors of huge rotting timber. A glossy arch of water slipped over this, crashed to the bottom, then poured along the ravine and flowed through open doors at the end into a small loch fringed with reeds and paved with lily leaves. Thaw knew this must be the canal, a dangerous forbidden place where children were drowned. He followed his companions uphill among structures where water spilled over ledges, trickled through cracks, or lay in rushy half-stagnant ponds with swans paddling on clear spaces in the middle. They crossed a plank bridge under the shadow of so high a waterfall that the din of it was deafening. They crossed stony ground and then another bridge and heard dimly a distant bugle blown in a caricature of a battle call.

"Peely Wally," said Boab.

They went quickly down a cinder path, through a gate and into a street.

Thaw found it a foreign kind of street. The tenements were faced with grey stone instead of red, landing windows had broken glass in them, or no glass, or even no window frames, being oblong holes half bricked up to stop children falling out. The men who had taken the spikes away to the war from Riddrie (where Thaw lived) had removed all the railings here, and the spaces between pavement and tenement (neat gardens in Riddrie) were spaces of flattened earth where children too young to walk scratched the ground with bent spoons or floated bits of wood in puddles left from last week's rain. In the middle of the street a pale lipless smiling young man sat on a donkey cart with a bugle on his knees. His cart held boxes of coloured toys which could be bought with rags, bottles and jam jars, and already a crowd of children surrounded him wearing cardboard sombreros, whooping on whistles or waving bright flags and windmills. When he noticed Boab and the pram he shouted, "Make way! Make way! Let the man through!"

While these two haggled Thaw and the smaller boys stood round the donkey and admired the mildness of its face, the hardness of its forehead and the white hair inside the trumpet-shaped ears. Thaw argued about the donkey's age with the boy wearing the hat.

"I bet ye a pound he's older than you onyway," said the boy.
"And I bet ye a pound he isnae."
"Why d'ye think he isnae?"
"Why d'ye think he is?"
"Peely!" shouted the boy. "How old is your donkey?"
"A hundred!" shouted Peely.
"There ye are—I wiz right!" said the boy. "Now you've tae give me a pound." He held his hand out, saying, "Come on now. Pay up!"
The children who had heard the argument whispered and giggled, and some beckoned friends who were standing at a distance. Thaw, frightened, said, "I havenae a pound."
"But ye promised! Didn't he promise?"
"Aye, he promised," said several voices. "He bet a pound."
"He's got to pay."
"I don't believe the donkey is a hundred," said Thaw.
"Ye think ye're awful clever, don't ye?" a thin girl shouted venomously and sarcastic voices cried, "Oh, Mammy, Mammy, I'm an awful smart wee boy."
"Why does the smart wee boy no' believe the donkey's a hundred?"
"Because I read it in an ENCYCLOPAEDIA," said Thaw, for though he was still unable to read he had once pleased his parents by saying encyclopaedia without being specially taught and the word had peculiar qualities for him. Pronounced in the service of his lie it had an immediate effect. Someone at the edge of the crowd jumped into the air, clapped hands above head and cried, "Oh, the big word! The big word!" and the mob exploded into laughter and mockery. Waving flags and blowing whistles, they raved and stamped around the frightened stone-still Thaw until his lips trembled and a drop of water spilled from his left eye.
"Look!" they yelled. "He's greeting!" "Crybaby! Crybaby!" "Cowardy custard, stick yer nose in the mustard!" "Riddrie pup with yer tail tied up!" "Awa' hame and tell yer mammy!" Thaw was blinded by red rage and screamed, "Buggers! Ye damned buggers!" and started running down the darkening street. He heard the clattering feet of pursuers and Peely Wally laugh like a cock-crow and Boab roar, "Let him go! Leave him alone!"
He turned a corner and ran down a street past staring children and men who paid no attention, through a small park with a pond and the sound of splashing water, then down a rutted lane, going slower because they weren't following now, with

longer intervals between his sobs. He sat down on a chunk of masonry and swallowed air until his heart beat more calmly.

There was empty ground in front of him with the shadows of tenements stretching a long way across it. Colours had become distinctions of grey and close-mouths' black rectangles in tenement walls. The sky was covered with blue-grey cloud, but currents of wind had opened channels through this and he could see through the channels into a green sunset air above. Down the broadest of these flew five swans on their way to a lower stretch of the canal or to a pond in the city parks.

Thaw started back the way he had come, sniffing and wiping tears from his nose. In the small dim park only the splashing of water was distinct. It was night in the streets. He was glad to see no children or grown people or any of the adolescent groups who usually gather by street corners at nightfall. Black lampposts stood at wide intervals on either kerb. The tenement windows were black like holes in a face. Twice he saw wardens cross the end of some street ahead, silent helmeted men examining blinded windows for illegal chinks of light. The dark, similar streets seemed endlessly to open out of each other until he despaired of getting home and sat on the kerb with his face in his hands and girned aloud. He fell into a dwam in which he felt only the hard kerb under his backside and awoke suddenly with a hushing sound in his ears. For a second this seemed like his mother singing to him then he recognized the noise of waterfalls. The sky had cleared and a startling moon had risen. Though not full there was enough of it to light the canal embankment across the road, and the gate, and the cinder path. He went gladly and fearfully to the gate and climbed the path with the hushing growing in his ears to the full thunder of the falling stream. Several trembling stars were reflected in the dark water below.

As he stepped off the bridge Thaw seemed to hear the moon yell at him. It was the siren. Its ululations came eerily across the rooftops to menace him, the only life. He ran down the path between the nettles and through the gate and past the dark allotments. The siren swooned into silence and a little later (Thaw had never heard this before) there was a dull iron noise, *gron-gron-gron-gron*, and dark shapes passed above him. Later there were abrupt thuddings as if giant fists were battering a metal ceiling over the city. Beams of light widened, narrowed

and groped above the rooftops, and between two tenements
he saw the horizon lit orange and red with irregular flashing
lights. Black flies seemed to be circling in the glow. Beyond
the power station he ran his head into the stomach of a warden
running the other way. "Duncan!" shouted the man.

Thaw was picked into the air and shaken.

"Where have ye been? Where have ye been? Where have ye
been?" shouted the man senselessly, and Thaw, full of love
and gratitude, shouted, "Daddy!"

Mr. Thaw tucked his son under one arm and ran back
home. Between the jolts of his father's strides Thaw heard
the iron noise again. They went up steps into the close-mouth
and Thaw was put down. They stood together in the dark,
breathing hard; then Mr. Thaw said in a weak voice Thaw
hardly recognized, "I suppose you know the worry you've given
your mother and me?"

There was a shriek and bang and pieces of dirt hit Thaw on
the cheek.

From the living-room window next morning he saw a hole
in the pavement across the street. The blast had shaken soot
down the chimney onto the living-room floor, and Mrs. Thaw
cleaned it up, stopping sometimes to talk with neighbours who
called to discuss the raid. They agreed that it might have been
worse, but Thaw was very uneasy. His adventure with the midden-rakers was a horrider crime than not eating dinner so he
expected punishment on an unusually large scale. After closely
watching his mother that day—noticing the way she hummed
to herself when dusting, her small thoughtful pauses in the
middle of work, her way of scolding when he was stupid during
a lesson on clock reading—he became sure that punishment
was not in her mind, and this worried him. He feared pain,
but deserved to be hurt, and was not going to be hurt. He
had not returned to exactly the same house.

CHAPTER 13. A Hostel

The house was changing. Obscure urgency filled it and in bed at night he heard rumours of preparation and debate. Coming home from a friend's back green he stuck with his head on one side of the railings and his body on the other. Mr. and Mrs. Thaw released him by greasing his ears with butter and pulling a leg each, laughing all the time. When free he flung himself howling on the grass but they tickled his armpits and sang "Stop Yer Ticklin', Jock" until he couldn't help laughing. Then one day they all came out onto the landing and the house was locked behind them. His father and mother carried his sister Ruth and some luggage; Thaw had a gas mask in a cardboard box hanging from his shoulder by a string loop; they all went up to his school by the sunlit bird-twittering back lanes. Murmuring groups of mothers stood in the playground with small children at their side. The fathers spoke in noisier groups and older children played halfheartedly between.

Thaw felt bored and walked to the railings. He was sure he was going on holiday and that holidays meant the sea. From the edge of the playground's high platform he looked across the canal and the Blackhill tenements to remote hills with a dip in the middle. Looking the opposite way he saw a wide valley of roofs and smokestacks with more hills beyond. These hills were nearer and greener and so distinct that along a gently curved summit a line of treetops joined like a hedge and he saw the sky between the trunks underneath. It struck him that the sea was behind these hills; if he stood among the trees he would look down on a grey sea sparkling with waves. His mother shouted his name and he strolled toward her slowly, pretending he had not heard but was returning anyway. She adjusted the string of the gas mask which had got across his coat collar and was cutting the side of his neck, then made the coat sit better on his shoulders with tugs and pats which shook his head from side to side. He said, "Is the sea behind there?"

"Behind where?"

"Behind where those trees are."

"Who told you that? Those are the Cathkin Braes. There's nothing behind there but farms and fields. And England, eventually."

The sparkling grey sea was too vivid for him to disbelieve. It fought in his head with a picture of farms and fields until it seemed to be flooding them. He pointed to the hills behind Blackhill and asked, "Is the sea over there?"

"No, but there's Loch Lomond and the highlands."

Mrs. Thaw stopped tidying him, lifted Ruth on her left arm and stared straight-backed at the Cathkin Braes. She said thoughtfully, "When I was a girl those trees reminded me of a caravan on the skyline."

"What's a caravan?"

"A procession of camels. In Arabia."

"What's a procession?"

Red single-decker buses suddenly came into the playground and everyone but the fathers climbed on board. Mr. and Mrs. Thaw said goodbye through the window and after a long wait the buses drove out of the playground and down to the Cumbernauld Road.

A dim broken time followed when Thaw and his mother, with Ruth on her lap, sat in buses at night hurling through unseen country. The buses were always badly lit with windows blinded by blue-black oilcloth so that nobody saw out. There must have been many such journeys, but later he remembered a single night journey lasting many months in a cabin full of hungry tired people, though the movement of the bus was interrupted by confused adventures in dim places: a wooden church hall, a room over a tailor's shop, a stone-floored kitchen with beetles crawling over it. He slept in strange beds where breathing became difficult and he woke up screaming he was dead. Sores appeared on his scrotum and the bus brought them to the Royal Infirmary where old professors looked between his legs and applied brown ointment which stung the sores and smelled of tar. The bus was always crowded, Ruth crying, his mother weary and Thaw bored, though once a drunk man stood up and embarrassed everyone by trying to get them to sing. Then one evening the bus stopped and they got out and met his father, who led them onto the deck of a ship. They stood in the dusk near the funnel which gave out comfortable heat. The air was cold between slate-dark clouds and a heaving slate-blue sea. A reef lay among the lapping water like a long black log, and at one end an iron tripod upheld a lit yellow globe. The ship moved out to sea.

They came to live in a bungalow among low concrete buildings called the hostel. This stood between sea and moorland. Munition workers slept there and it held a canteen, cinema and hospital and had a high wire fence all round with gates that were locked at night. Each morning Thaw and Ruth were taken in a car along the coast road to the village school. This had two classrooms and a kitchen where a wife from the village made flavourless meals. A headmaster called Macrae taught the older pupils and a woman called Ingram the small ones. The pupils were all children of crofters excepting some evacuees from Glasgow who lodged in farms on the moors.

On his first day in the new school the other boys rushed to be Thaw's neighbour in the queue to go out to play, and in the playfield they gathered round to ask where he came from and what his father did. Thaw answered truthfully at first but later told lies to keep their interest. He said he spoke several languages and when asked to prove this could only say that "wee" was French for "yes." Most of the group went away after that, and next day in the playfield he had an audience of two. To stop it getting smaller he offered to show them round the hostel, then other boys approached him in threes and fours and asked if they could come too. Instead of going home that night in the car with Ruth, Thaw trudged along the coast road at the head of a mob of thirty or forty who talked and joked with each other and, apart from an occasional question, totally ignored him. He was not sorry about this. He wanted to seem mysterious to these boys, someone ageless with strange powers, but his feet were sore, he was late for tea and afraid he would be blamed for arriving with so many friends. He was right. The hostel gateman refused to allow the other boys in. They had walked two miles and missed their tea to accompany him and though he walked back with them a little way apologizing they were still very angry and the evacuees began to throw stones. He ran back to the hostel where he was given a cold meal and a row for "showing off."

Next morning he pretended to be ill but unluckily the asthma and the disease between his legs weren't troublesome and he had to go to school. Nobody spoke to him there and at playtime he kept nervously to the field's quietest corner. On queuing to re-enter the classroom he stood beside an evacuee called Coulter who pushed him in the side. Thaw pushed back. Coulter punched him in the side, Thaw punched back and Coulter muttered, "A'll see you after school."

Thaw said, "A've to go straight home after school tonight; my dad said so."

"Right. I'll see ye the morra."

At home that night he refused to eat anything. He said, "I've a pain."

"You don't *look* sick," said Mrs. Thaw. "Where *is* the pain?"

"All over."

"What kind of pain is it?"

"I don't know, but I'm not going to school tomorrow."

Mrs. Thaw said to her husband, "You deal with this, Duncan, it's beyond me."

Mr. Thaw took his son into the bedroom and said, "Duncan, there's something you haven't told us."

Thaw started crying and said what the matter was. His father held him to his chest and asked, "Is he bigger than you?"

"Yes." (This was untrue.)

"Much bigger?"

"No," said Thaw after a fight with his conscience.

"Do you want me to ask Mr. Macrae to tell the other pupils not to hit you?"

"No," said Thaw, who only wanted not to go to school.

"I knew you would say that, Duncan. Duncan, you'll have to fight this boy. If ye start running away now you'll never learn to face up to life. I'll teach ye how to fight—it's easy—all ye have to do is use your left hand to protect your face. . . ."

Mr. Thaw talked like this until Thaw's head was full of images of defeating Coulter. He spent that evening practising for the fight. First he sparred with his father, but the opposition of a real human being left no scope for fantasy, so he practised on a cushion and went confidently to bed after a good supper.

He was less confident next morning and ate breakfast very
quietly. Mrs. Thaw kissed him goodbye and said, "Don't worry.
You'll knock his block off."
She waved encouragingly as the car drove away.

That morning Thaw stood in a lonely corner of the playfield
and waited fearfully for the approach of Coulter, who was playing football with friends. Rain started falling and gradually
the pupils collected in a shelter at the end of the building.
Thaw was last to enter. In an agony of dread he walked up
to Coulter, stuck his tongue out at him and struck him on
the shoulder. At once they started fighting as unskilfully as
small boys always fight, with flailing arms and a tendency to
kick each other's ankles; then they grappled and fell. Thaw
was beneath but Coulter's nose flattened on his brow, the result-
ing blood smeared both equally, each thought it his own and,
appalled by the suspected wound, rolled apart and stood up.
After that, in spite of encouragement from their allies (Thaw
was surprised to find a cheering mob of allies at his back)
they were content to stand swearing at each other until Miss
Ingram came up and took them to the headmaster. Mr. Macrae
was a stout pig-coloured man. He said, "Right. What's the
cause of all this?"
Thaw started talking rapidly, his explanation punctuated by
gulps and stutters, and only stopped when he found himself
starting to sob. Coulter said nothing. Mr. Macrae took a leather
tawse from his desk and said, "Hold your hands out."
Each held his hand out and got a hellish stinging wallop on
it. Mr. Macrae said, "Again!" "Again!" and "Again!" Then
he said, "If I hear of you two fighting another time you'll
get the same treatment but more of it, a lot more of it. Go
to your class."
Each bent his head to hide his distorted face and went to the
next room sucking a crippled hand. Miss Ingram didn't ask
them to do anything for the rest of the morning.

After the fight Thaw found playtimes more boring than
frightening. He would stand in the lonely corner of the field
with a boy called McLusky who didn't play with the other
boys because he was feebleminded. Thaw told long stories with
himself as hero and McLusky helped him mime the actable
bits. The vivid part of his life became imaginary. Thaw and
his sister slept in adjacent rooms, and at night he told her
stories through the doorway between, stories with the adven-

tures and landscapes of books he had read by day. Sometimes
he stopped and asked, "Are you asleep yet? Will I go on?"
and Ruth answered, "No, Duncan, please go on," but at last
she would fall asleep. Next night she would say, "Go on with
the story, Duncan."

"All right. Where did I stop last night?"

"They . . . they had landed on Venus."

"No, no. They had left Venus and gone to Mercury."

"I . . . don't remember that, Duncan."

"Of course you don't. Ye fell asleep. Well, I'm not going to
tell *you* stories if you don't want to listen."

"But I couldnae help falling asleep, Duncan."

"Then why didn't ye tell me you were falling asleep instead
of letting me go on talking to myself?"

After bullying her some more he would continue the story,
for he spent a lot of time each day preparing it.

He bullied Ruth in other ways. She was forbidden to stott
her ball indoors. He saw her do it once, and terrified her for
weeks by threatening to tell their mother. One day Mrs. Thaw
accused her children of stealing sugar from the livingroom sideboard. Both denied it. Later Ruth told him, "you stole that
sugar."

He said "yes. But if you tell Mum I said so I'll call you a
liar and she won't know who to believe." Ruth at once told
their mother, Thaw called Ruth a liar, and Mrs. Thaw didn't
know who to believe.

During the first few weeks at school he had looked carefully
among the girls for one to adventure with in his imagination,
but they were all too obviously the same vulgar clay as himself.
For almost a year he resigned himself to loving Miss Ingram,
who was moderately attractive and whose authority gave her
a sort of grandeur. Then one day when visiting the village
store he saw a placard in the window advertising Amazon Adhesive Shoe Soles. It showed a blond girl in brief Greek armour
with spear and shield and a helmet on her head. Above her
were the words BEAUTY PLUS STAMINA, and her face had
a plaintive loveliness which made Miss Ingram seem commonplace. During the dinner intervals Thaw walked to the store
and looked at the girl for the length of time it took to count
ten. He knew that by looking too hard and often even she
might come to seem commonplace.

CHAPTER 14. Ben Rua

Mr. Thaw wanted a keener intimacy with his son and liked open-air activities. There were fine mountains near the hostel, the nearest of them, Ben Rua, less than sixteen hundred feet high; he decided to take Thaw on some easy excursions and bought him stout climbing boots. Unluckily Thaw wanted to wear sandals.

"I like to move my toes," he said.

"What are ye blethering about?"

"I don't like shutting my feet in these hard solid leather cases. It makes them feel dead. I can't bend my ankles."

"But you arenae supposed to bend your ankles! It's the easiest thing in the world to break an ankle if you slip in an awkward place. These boots are made especially to give the ankle support—once a single nail gets a grip it can uphold your ankle, your leg, your whole body even."

"What I lose in firmness I'll make up in quickness."

"I see. I see. For a century mountaineers have gone up the Alps and Himalayas and Grampians in nailed climbing boots. You might think they knew about climbing. Oh, no, Duncan Thaw knows better. They should have worn *sandals.*"

"What's wrong for them might be right for me."

"My God!" cried Mr. Thaw. "What's this I've brought into the world? What did I do to deserve this? If we could only live by our own experience we would have no science, no civilization, no progress! Man has advanced by his capacity to learn from others, and these boots cost me four pounds eight."

"There would be no science and civilization and all that if everybody did things the way everybody else does," said Thaw. The discussion continued until Mr. Thaw lost his temper and Thaw had hysterics and was given a cold bath. The climbing boots lay in a cupboard until Ruth was old enough to use them. Meanwhile Thaw was not taken climbing by his father.

One summer day Thaw walked briskly along the coast road until the hostel was hidden by a green headland. It was a sunny afternoon. A few clouds lay about the sky like shirts scattered on a blue floor. He left the road and ran down a slope toward the sea, his feet crashing almost to the ankles among pebbles and shells. He felt confident and resolute, for he had been reading a book called *The Young Naturalist* and meant to make notes of anything interesting. The shingle gave onto shelving rocks with boulders and pools among them. He squatted by a pool the size of a soup plate and peered in, frowning. Below the crystalline water lay three pebbles, a small anemone the colour of raw liver, a wisp of green weed and several winkles. The winkles were olive and dull purple, and he thought he saw a tendency for the pale ones to be at the edges of the pool and the dark ones in the middle. Taking out a notebook and pencil he drew a map on the blank first page, showing the position of the winkles; then he wrote the date on the opposite page and added after some thought the letters:

SELKNIW ELPRUP NI ECIDRAWOC

for he wished to hide his discoveries under a code until he was ready to publish. Then he pocketed the notebook and strolled onto a beach of smooth white sand lapped by the sparkling sea. Tired of being a naturalist he found a stick of driftwood and began engraving the plans of a castle on the firm surface. It was a very elaborate castle full of secret entrances, dungeons and torture chambers.

Someone behind him said, "What's that supposed to be?" Thaw turned and saw Coulter. He gripped the stick tightly and muttered, "It's some plans."
Coulter walked round the plans saying, "What are they plans of?"
"Oh, they're just plans."
"Well, mibby you're wise no' to tell me what they're plans of. For all you know I'm mibby a German spy."
"You couldnae be a German spy."
"Yes I could."
"You're just a boy!"
"But mibby the Germans have a secret chemical that stops

folk growing so they look like boys though they're mibby twenty or thirty, and mibby they've landed me here off a submarine and I'm just pretending to be an evacuee but all the time I'm spying on the hostel your dad is managing."

Thaw stared at Coulter who stood with feet apart and hands in trouser pockets and stared back. Thaw said, *"Are* you a German spy?"

"Yes," said Coulter.

His face was so expressionless that Thaw became convinced that he was a German spy. At the same time, without noticing it, he had stopped being afraid of Coulter. He said, "Well I'm a British spy."

"You are not."

"I am so."

"Prove it."

"Prove you're a German spy."

"I don't want to. If I did you could get me arrested and hung."

Thaw could think of no answer to this. He was wondering how to make Coulter think he was a British spy when Coulter said, "Do you come from Glasgow?"

"Yes!"

"So do I."

"What bit of Glasgow?"

"Garngad. What bit do you come from?"

"Riddrie."

"Hm! Riddrie is quite near Garngad. They're both on the canal."

Coulter looked at the plans again and said, "Is it a plan of a den?"

"Well . . . a sort of den."

"I know some smashing dens."

"So do I!" said Thaw eagerly. "I've got a den inside a—"

"I've got a den that's a real secret cave!" said Coulter triumphantly.

Thaw was impressed. After a suitable silence he said, *"My* den is inside a bush. It looks like an ordinary bush outside but it's all hollow inside and it stands beside this road in the hostel so you can sit in it and watch these daft munition girls passing and they don't know you're there. The bother is"—truth made him reluctantly add—"it doesnae keep out the rain."

"That's the bother with dens," said Coulter. "Either they're secret and let in rain or they don't let in rain and arenae secret. My cave keeps the rain out fine, but last time I went there the floor was all covered with dirty straw. I think the tinkers

had been using it. But I could make a great den if I had somebody to help me."

"How?"

"Will ye promise no' to tell anyone?"

"Aye, sure."

"It's up a place near the hotel."

They crossed the beach to the road and walked along it chatting
amiably.

Before reaching the village they turned up a track which
ascended to the tall iron gates and yew trees of the Kinlochrua Hotel. Past this the track became a path half covered
by bracken. It led them precariously higher and higher between
boulders and bushes until Coulter halted and said triumphantly,
"There!"

They were on the lip of a gully sloping down to the waters
of the burn. It had been used as a rubbish dump and was
half filled by an avalanche of tins, broken crockery, cinders
and decaying cloth. Thaw looked at it with pleasure and said,
"Aye, there's plenty of stuff here for a den."

"Let's get out the big cans first," said Coulter.

They waded among the rubbish, collecting materials, then carried them to a flat place beneath two big rocks. They used
petrol drums for the walls of the den and roofed it with linoleum
laid across wooden spars. They were finishing by stuffing odd
holes with sacking when Thaw heard a footstep and looked
around. A shepherd was passing downhill waist deep in the
bracken to their left. "Good afternoon, lads," he said.

Thaw began working more and more slowly. Until then he
had been chatting enthusiastically, now he became silent and
answered questions as shortly as possible. At last Coulter threw
down a piece of pipe he had been trying to make into a chimney
and said, "What's wrong with ye?"

"This den's no use. It's too near the path. Everybody can see
it. It's not secret at all."

Coulter glared at Thaw then gripped the linoleum roof,
wrenched it off and threw it down the gully.

"What are ye doing?" shouted Thaw.

"It's no use! Ye said so yourself! I'm taking it down!"

Coulter pushed down the walls and kicked the drums into the
gulley. Thaw watched sullenly until nothing was left but a few
spars of wood and a distant clanking sound. He said, "Ye neednae have done that. We might have camouflaged it with
branches and stuff and hidden it that way."

Coulter shoved through the bracken to the path and started
walking down it. After a few yards he turned and shouted,
"Ye bugger! Ye damned bugger!"
"Ye bloody damned bugger!" shouted Thaw.
"Ye *fuckin'* bloody damned bugger!" yelled Coulter, and disappeared from sight among the trees. Brooding blackly on the
den, which had been a good one, Thaw walked up the track
in the opposite direction.

The glen had taken all the streams of the moor into its
gorge where they tumbled and clattered among boulders, leaves
and the songs of blackbirds, but Thaw paid little attention to
the surroundings. His thoughts took on a pleasant flavour. Expressions of grimness, mockery and excitement crossed his face
and sometimes he waved an arm imperiously. Once he said
with a bleak smile, "I'm sorry, madam, but you fail to understand your position. You are my prisoner."
It was a while before he noticed he had left the glen behind
but there was an uneasiness in the quiet of the open moor
which daydreams couldn't shut out. The main sound was the
water flowing clear and brown, golden brown where the sun
caught it, along runnels which could have been bridged by a
hand. In places the heather had knotted its twigs and roots
across these and it was possible to follow their course by a
melodious gurgling under the purple-green carpet which sloped
and dipped upward to the humps and boulders of Ben Rua.
Thaw suddenly saw himself as if from the sky, a small figure
starting across the moor like a louse up a quilt. He stood still
and gazed at the ben. On the grey-green tip of the summit
he seemed just able to see a figure, a vertical white speck that
moved and gestured, though the movement might have been
caused by a flickering of warm air between the mountaintop
and his eye. To Thaw the movement suggested a woman in
a white dress waving and beckoning. He could even imagine
her face: it was the face of the girl in the adhesive shoe-sole
advertisement. This remote beckoning woman struck him with
the force of a belief, though it was not quite a belief. He
did not decide to climb the mountain, he thought, 'I'll follow this bit of stream,' or, 'I'll go to the rock over there.'
And he would reach the top of a slope to find a higher one
beyond and the ben looking nearer each time. Sometimes
he climbed on a boulder and stood for minutes listening to
small noises which might have been the distant scrape of a
sheep's hoof on a stone, or the scutter of a rabbit's paw, or

the fluttering of blood in his eardrum. From these pedestals the summit of Rua sometimes looked vacant, but later, with a pang, he would see on it the flickering white point. He advanced onto the mountain slope and the summit passed out of sight.

The lower slopes were mostly widths of granite tilted at the angle of the mountainside, level with the heather and cracked like the pavements of a ruined city. Higher up the heather gave way to fine turf, where grasshoppers chirped and flowerets grew with stalks less than an inch high and blossoms hardly bigger than pinheads. Becoming thirsty he found a shallow pool collected from last week's rain in the hollow of a rock. Stopping to drink he felt rough granite under his lips and warm sour water on the tongue. The mountain steepened into nearly vertical blocks with ledges of turf between. For half an hour he used his hands as much as his feet, squirming and wriggling up crooked funnels, pulling himself over small precipices, then lying flat on his back on a ledge under the shadow of the summit to let the sweat dry out of his damp shirt. At this height he heard noises that had been shut off from him on the moor: a barking dog on one of the farms, a door slamming in the hostel, a lark above a field behind the village, children shouting on the shore and the murmuring sea. He contained two equal sorts of knowledge: the warm lazy knowledge that above on the mountain a blond girl in a white dress waited for him, shy and eager; and the cooler knowledge that this was unlikely and the good of climbing was the exercise and view from the top. There was no conflict between those knowledges, his mind passed easily from one to the other, but when he stood up to begin the last of the climb the thought of the girl was stronger.

He was at the foot of a granite cliff about four times his height with a ledge sloping up it made by a lower stratum projecting beyond the one above. As he climbed his fear of height made the excitement keener. The ledge was decayed and gravelly, each step sent a shower of little lumps rattling and bouncing down into the sky beyond the edge. Gradually it narrowed to a few inches. Thaw pressed his chest against the granite, stood on tiptoe and, reaching up, brought his fingertips within an inch of the top. "Hell, hell, hell, hell, hell," he muttered sadly, gazing at the dark rock where it cut against a white smudge of cloud. A face suddenly stuck over this edge and looked down at him. It was a small, round, wrinkled almost sexless face, and the shock of it nearly made Thaw lose balance. It took him a moment to recognize Mr. McPhedron, the minister from the village. The minister said, "Are you stuck?"

"No, I can go back."

"Aye. The right way up is round the other side. But bide there a minute."

The face was withdrawn and Thaw saw something black and straight with a curled end poke over the edge and slide toward him. It was the handle of an umbrella. Swallowing the fear that slid up his gullet Thaw gripped the handle with his left hand and tugged. It stayed firm. He put the toe of his sandal against a bump in the rock face, gripped the handle tighter, heaved himself at the edge and got an arm across. The arm was grabbed and he was pulled onto the summit. He sat up and said, "Thank you."

The summit was a rock platform as big as the floor of a room and tilted so that one side was higher than the others. On the highest corner stood a squat concrete pillar like a steep pyramid with the top cut off. With a sad pang he saw that this had seemed the beckoning white woman. The minister, a bald dry little man in crumpled black clothes, sat nearby with his legs over the edge, fists resting on thighs and back as upright as if sitting in a chair. The rolled umbrella lay behind him. He turned and said, "Now you have your breath back, give me your opinion of the view."

Thaw stood up. The moor lay below with dots of sheep grazing on it, some shrub-filled glens and the green coastal strip beyond. The village was hidden by the trees of the largest glen but its position was shown by the hotel roof among its conifers and by the end of a pier sticking into the Atlantic. To the left of this, between the beach and the white road, the hostel stood in neat rectangular blocks like a chess game, human specks moving on the straight paths between. Farther off still, the road—a bus moving down it like an insect—turned from the coast into a district of moorland with small lochs and blue-grey bens paling into the distance like waves of a stone sea. The ocean in front, however, was as shining-smooth as slightly wrinkled silk. It stretched to the dark mountains of the Isle of Skye on the horizon, and the sun hung above these at the height of Thaw himself. It was dimmed and oranged by haze but firing golden wires of light from the centre. Thaw stared at it miserably. The minister was someone he tried to avoid. On coming to the hostel his mother, who went to church, sent him to a Sunday school held by Dr. McPhedron after the morning service. He had expected to sing little hymns and draw little pictures of Bible stories; instead he was given a book of questions and answers to learn by heart so that when Dr. McPhedron asked a question like "Why did God make man?" Thaw could give an answer like "God made man to glorify his name and enjoy his works for ever." After the first day of Sunday school he didn't want to go back and his father, who was an atheist, said he needn't if he didn't enjoy it. Since then Thaw had heard his parents discuss the minister several times. His mother said there was too much Hell in his sermons. She thought churches were good because they gave people something to look up to and hope for, but she didn't believe in Hell and it was wrong to frighten children with it. Mr. Thaw said he saw no reason why people shouldn't believe what pleased them but McPhedron was a type found too often in the highlands and islands, a bigot who damned to Hell whoever rejected his narrow opinions.

To hide embarrassment Thaw turned and examined the pillar.
"Do you wonder what that is, now?" asked the minister. His voice was soft and precise.
"Yes."
"It is a triangulation point. Your name is still on my Sunday school enrolment book. Would you have me remove it?"
Thaw frowned and rubbed his fingers round an odd depression in the pillar's top.
The minister said, *"That* is to hold the base of an instrument used by government mapmakers. I notice you don't come to kirk with your mother any more. Why?"
"Dad says I needn't go to something I don't like if it isn't educational," muttered Thaw. The minister gave a slight friendly laugh.
"I admire your father. His notion of education embraces everything but the purpose of life and the fate of man. Do you believe in the Almighty?"
Thaw said boldly, "I don't know, but I don't believe in Hell."
The minister laughed again. "When you have more knowledge of life you will mibby find Hell more believable. You are from Glasgow?"

"Yes."

"I was six years a student of divinity in that city. It made Hell very real to me."

A muffled blast came to their ears from a distance. A white cloud drifted up from a dip in the moorlands to the south, shredding and vanishing as it rose. The sound was batted back and forth between the mountains, then trickled into echoes among far off glens.

"Yes," said the minister. "They are testing at the munition factory down there. The country must be preserved with all the Hell we can muster."

Thaw was filled with baffled anger. He had bitten into the splendid fruit of the afternoon and found a core of harsh dull words. He muttered that he'd better be getting home.

"Aye," said the minister. "It is late for a wee lad to be far from bed."

He got up and led Thaw from the summit by a fall of granite blocks which presented so many horizontal surfaces that he went down it like a flight of giant steps, hopping nimbly from one to another, using the umbrella to balance him in awkward places. Thaw jumped and scrambled sullenly after him. When they reached the more grassy slopes Thaw let the distance between them increase until the minister vanished behind a boulder; then he turned left and scrambled round the mountainside until a sufficient girth of it was between them and then set off toward the hostel.

The sun had set by the time he reached the road but it was still the gloaming, a protracted summer gloaming with the land dim but the sky lively with colours. He limped in at the hostel gate, the hard tarmac hurting his feet, and went by two straight paths to the manager's bungalow. His mother sat knitting on a deck chair on the lawn. Nearby his father stabbed casually with a hoe at weeds in a small rockery. As Thaw approached Mrs. Thaw called reprovingly, "We were beginning to worry about you!"

He had meant to keep quiet about the climb as he had made it wearing sandals, but standing between his parents he said, "I bet you don't know where I've been!"

"Well, where have you been?"

"There!"

Behind the hostel's low straight roofs Rua showed like a black wedge cut out of the green rotund-looking sky. Soft stars were beginning to shine between a few feathery bloody clouds.

"You were up Ben Rua?"

"Aye."

"Alone?"

"Aye."

His mother said gently, "That could have been dangerous, Duncan."

His father looked at his sandalled feet and said, "If you do it again you must tell someone you're going first, so we know where to look if there's an accident. But I don't think we'll complain this time; no, we won't complain, we won't complain."

CHAPTER 15. Normal

The Thaw family came home to Glasgow the year the war ended.
They arrived late at night as thin rain fell, took a taxi at the
station and sat numbly inside. Thaw looked out at a succession
of desolate streets lit by lights that seemed both dim and harsh.
Once Glasgow had been a tenement block, a school and a
stretch of canal; now it was a gloomy huge labyrinth he would
take years to find a way through. The flat was cold and disordered. During the war it had been let to strangers and the
bedding and ornaments locked in the back bedroom. While
his father and mother unpacked and shifted things he looked
at his old books and found them dull and childish. He asked
his mother, who was dusting, "How long will it be before
we get back to normal?"
"What do you mean, normal?"
"You know, settled down."
"I suppose in a week or two."
He went to the living room where his father was looking
through letters and said, "How long will it be before we get
back to normal?"
"Maybe in two or three months, if we're lucky."

Mr. Thaw spent the next months typing letters at his bureau
in the living room. With each post he got back letters with
printed headings which he gave to Thaw, who drew on the
blank backs. Thaw sat drawing and writing for hours at a tiny
desk in the back bedroom, wearing a dressing gown and an
embroidered smoking cap which had been his grandfather's.
He seldom looked at the letters whose backs he used, but once
his eye was caught by the heading of the factory where his
father had worked before the war. He read:

Dear Mr Thaw,

It would seem that a prophet is not without honour save in the city of his birth! I congratulate you on having done so well with the now defunct Ministry of Munitions.

Unfortunately we have no vacancy for a personnel officer at present. However, I am sure your manifest abilities will have no difficulty in finding employment elsewhere. Our hearty good wishes to you.

Yours faithfully,

John Blair

Managing Director

One day at dinner Mr. Thaw said to his wife, "I took a walk out Hogganfield way this morning. They're building a reservoir to serve the new housing scheme." He swallowed a mouthful and said, "I went in and got a job. I start tomorrow."

"What doing?"

"The walls of the reservoir are made by pouring concrete between metal shuttering. I'll be bolting the shutters into place and taking them down when the stuff has hardened."

Mrs. Thaw said grimly, "It's better than nothing."

"That's what I thought."

After this Mr. Thaw cycled to work each morning wearing an old jacket and corduroy trousers tucked into his stocking tops, and now when Thaw was not at school he scribbled at Mr. Thaw's bureau or lay reading on the hearth rug, enjoying his mother's proximity as she went about the housework.

One day Mr. Thaw said, "Duncan, you sit your qualifying exam in six weeks, don't you?"

"Yes."

"You realize how important this exam is? If you pass you'll go to a senior secondary school where, if you work well at your lessons and homework and pass the proper exams, you'll be able to take your Higher Leaving Certificates and work at anything you like. You can even do another four years at university. If you fail the qualifying exam you'll have to go to a junior secondary school and leave at fourteen and take any job you can get. Look at me. I went to a senior secondary school but I had to leave at fourteen to support my mother and sister. I think I had the ability to do well in life, but to do well you need certificates, certificates, and I had no certificates. The best I could become was a machine minder in Laird's box-making factory. During the war of course there was a short-

age of men with certificates, and I got a job purely on my
abilities. But look what I'm doing now. Have you any notion
of what you would like to be?''
Thaw considered. In the past he had wanted to be a king,
magician, explorer, archaeologist, astronomer, inventor and pi-
lot of spaceships. More recently, while scribbling in the back
bedroom, he had thought of writing stories or painting pictures.
He hesitated and said, ''A doctor.''
''A doctor! Yes, that's a good thing to be. A doctor gives his
life to helping others. A doctor is always, and will always be,
respected and needed by the community, no matter what social
changes take place. Well, your first step is the qualifying exam.
Don't worry about anything but that first step. You're good
at English and General Knowledge but bad at Arithmetic, so
what you must do is stick in at Arithmetic.'' Mr. Thaw patted
his son's back. ''Go to it!'' he said. Thaw went to his bedroom,
shut the door, lay on the bed and started crying. The future
his father indicated seemed absolutely repulsive.

Whitehill Senior Secondary School was a tall gloomy red
sandstone building with a playing field at the back and on each
side a square playground, one for each sex, enclosed and mini-
mized by walls with spiked railings on top. It had been built
like this in the eighteen-eighties but the growth of Glasgow
had imposed additions. A structure, outwardly uniform with
the old building but a warren of crooked stairs and small classrooms within, was stuck to the side at the turn of the century.
After the first world war a long wooden annexe was added
as temporary accommodation until a new school could be built,
and after the second world war, as a further temporary measure,
seven prefabricated huts holding two classrooms each were put
up on the playing field. On a grey morning some new boys
stood in a lost-looking crowd near the entrance gate. In primary
school they had been the playground giants. Now they were
dwarfs among a mob of people up to eighteen inches taller
than themselves. A furtive knot from Riddrie huddled together
trying to seem blasé. One said to Thaw, ''What are ye taking,
Latin or French?''
''French.''
''I'm taking Latin. Ye need it tae get to university.''
''But Latin's a dead language!'' said Thaw. ''My mother wants
me to take Latin but I tell her there are more good books in
French. And ye can use French tae travel.''
''Aye, mibby, but ye need Latin tae get to university.''

An electric bell screeched and a fat bald man in a black gown appeared on the steps of the main entrance. He stood with hands deep in his trouser pockets and feet apart, contemplating the buttons of his waistcoat while the older pupils hurried into lines before several entrances. One or two lines kept up a vague chatter and shuffle; he looked sternly at these and they fell silent. He motioned each class to the entrances one after another with a finger of his right hand. Then he beckoned the little group by the gate to the foot of the steps, lined them up, read their names from a list and led them into the building. The gloom of the entrance steeped them, then the dim light of echoing hall, then the cold light of a classroom.

Thaw entered last and found the only seat left was the undesirable one in the front row in front of the teacher, who sat behind a tall desk with his hands clasped on the lid. When everyone was seated he looked from left to right along the rows of faces before him, as if memorizing each one, then leaned back and said casually, "Now we'll divide you into classes. In the first year, of course, the only real division is between those who take Latin and those whos take . . . a modern language. At the end of the third year you will have to choose between other subjects: Geography or History, for instance; Science or Art; for by then you will be specializing for your future career. Hands up those who don't know what specializing means. No hands? Good. Your choice today is a simpler one, but its effects reach further. You all know Latin is needed for entrance to university. A number of benevolent people think this unfair and are trying to change it. As far as Glasgow University is concerned they haven't succeeded *yet."* He smiled an inward-looking smile and leaned back until he seemed to be staring at the ceiling. He said, "My name's Walkenshaw. I'm senior Classics master. Classics. That's what we call the study of Latin and Greek. Perhaps you've heard the word before? Who hasn't heard of classical music? Put your hand up if you haven't heard of classical music. No hands? Good. Classical music, you see, is the *best* sort of music, music by the best composers. In the same way the study of Classics is the study of the *best.* Are you chewing something?"

Thaw, who had been swallowing nervously, was appalled to find this question fired at himself. Not daring to take his gaze from the teacher's face he stood slowly up and shook his head.

"Answer me."

"No sir."

"Open your mouth. Open it wide. Stick your tongue out."
Thaw did as he was told. Mr. Walkenshaw leaned forward,
stared, then said mildly, "Your name?"
"Thaw, sir."
"That's all right, Thaw. You can sit down. And always tell
the truth, Thaw."
Mr. Walkenshaw leaned back and said, "Classics. Or, as we
call it at university, the Humanities. I say nothing against the
study of modern languages. Naturally half of you will choose
French. But Whitehall Senior Secondary School has a tradition,
a fine tradition of Classical scholarship, and I hope many of
you will continue that tradition. To those without enough ambi-
tion to go to university and who can't see the use of Latin, I
can only repeat the words of Robert Burns: 'Man cannot live
by bread alone.' No, and you would be wise to remember it.
Now I'm going to read your names again and I want you to
shout Modern and Classics according to choice."
He read the list of names again. Thaw was depressed to hear
all the people he knew choose Latin. He chose Latin.

The Latin students queued at the door of another classroom
opening out of the hall. The girls who had chosen Latin were
already there, giggling and whispering. It took Thaw a second
to notice and fall in love with the loveliest of them. She was
blond and wore a light dress, so he looked loftily round the
hall with an absent-minded frown hoping she would notice
his superior indifference. The hall was like an aquarium tank,
the light slanted into it from windows in the roof. On a wall
at one end a marble tablet showed a knight in Roman armour
and the names of pupils killed in the first world war. Photographs of headmasters hung between surrounding doors:
shaggy bearded early ones and neatly moustached recent ones,
but all with stern brows and clenched mouths. From a balcony
above came the horrible detonation of a leather belt striking
a hand. Somewhere a door opened and a voice said querulously,
"Marcellus animadvertit, Marcellus noticed this thing, and at once
into battle line formed the forces, and did not reluctantly, er
reluctantly take the opportunity of recalling to them how often
in the past they had borne themselves, er, nobly. . . ."

A lank young teacher led them into the classroom. The
girls sat in desks to his right, the boys to the left, and he faced
them with hands on hips leaning forward from the waist. He
said, "My name is Maxwell. I'm your form teacher. You come

to me first period each day to have the class register called
and to bring reasons for having been absent or late. They'd
better be good reasons. I'm also your Latin teacher."
He stared at them a while, then said, "I'm new to teaching.
Just as I'm your first senior secondary school teacher, you are
my first senior secondary school class. We're starting together,
you see, and I think we'd better decide here and now to start
well. You do right by me and I'll do right by you. But if we
quarrel about anything *you're* going to suffer. Not me."
He stared at them brightly and the frightened class stared back.
He had a craggy face with a rugged nose, trimmed red moustache and broad lips. Thaw noticed the undersurface of the
moustache was clipped to exactly continue the flat surface of
the upper lip. This detail frightened him even more than the
grim, nervous little speech.

Through the morning depression gathered in his brain
and chest like a physical weight. Each forty minutes the bell
screeched and the class moved to a different room and were
welcomed by a few unfriendly words. The Mathematics teacher
was a small brisk woman who said if they tried hard she would
help them all she could, but one thing she could not and would
not stand was dreaming. There was no room for dreamers in
her class. She gave out algebra and geometry books in which
Thaw saw a land without colour, furniture or action where
thought negotiated symbolically with itself. The science room
had a pungent chemical smell and shelves of strange objects
which excited his appetite for magic, but the teacher was a
big bullying man with hair like a beast's fur and Thaw knew
nothing *he* taught would bring an increase of power or freedom.
The art teacher was mild and middle-aged. He talked about
the laws of perspective, and how these laws had to be learned
before true art became possible. He gave out pencils and got
them to copy a wooden block onto a small sheet of paper. In
each class Thaw sat in the front row and stared at the teacher's
face. He was in a world where he could not do well, and he
wanted to give an impression of obedience that would make
the authorities treat him leniently. All the time he felt the pale
blaze of the blond girl somewhere behind him on the left.
Twice he dropped a book as an excuse for looking at her while
he picked it up. She seemed an unstill flickering girl, always
moving her shoulders, shaking her head and hair, smiling and
glancing from side to side. He noticed with surprise that her
oval face had a thrust-forward, slightly clumsy jaw. Her beauty

lay more in the movement of her parts than the parts themselves, which was maybe why she was never still.

The boys from Riddrie stood chattering in a queue for the tram which would take them home at noontime. One said, "That big Maxwell—I hate him. He looks mad enough to murder ye."

"Ach, naw, he'll be all right if ye do as he says. It's the science man I'm feart from. He's the sort that'll hammer ye jist because he's in a bad mood."

"Ach, they're all out to terrorize us today. The theory is that if they scare us enough at the start we'll give them nae trouble later. They've got a hope."

There was a reflective silence; then somebody said, "What dae ye think of the talent?"

"I care for that wee blond bird."

"Aye, did ye see her? She couldnae keep still. I wouldnae mind feeling *her* belly in a dark room."

Everyone but Thaw sniggered. Someone nudged him and said, "What do you think of her, moon-man?"

"Her jaw's too ape-like for me."

"Is it? All right. But I wouldnae give her back if I got her in a present. Does anyone know her name?

"I do. It's Kate Caldwell."

Things improved in the afternoon for they had English and the teacher was a young man with a comforting likeness to the film comedian Bob Hope. Without any introductory speech he said, "Today is the last day for handing in contributions for the school magazine. I'll give you paper and you can try to write something for it. It can be prose or poetry, serious or comic, an invented story or something that really happened. It doesn't matter if the result isn't up to much, but maybe one or two of you will get something accepted."

Thaw leaned over the paper, elated thoughts flowing through his head. His heart began to beat faster and he started writing. He quickly filled two sheets of foolscap then copied the result out carefully, checking the hard words with a dictionary. The teacher collected the papers and the bell rang for the next lesson.

Next day the class had geometry. The Maths teacher talked lucidly and drew clear diagrams on the blackboard, and Thaw gazed at her, trying by intensity of expression to make up for inability to understand. A girl came in and said, "Please, miss, Mister Meikle wants tae see Duncan Thaw in room fifty-four." As she led him across the playground to the wooden annexe, Thaw said, "Who's Mr. Meikle?"

"Head English teacher."

"What does he want me for?"

"How should I know?"

In room fifty-four a saturnine man in an academic gown leaned on a desk overlooking empty rows of desks. He turned toward Thaw a face that was long, lined and triangular under the oval of a balding skull. He had a small black moustache and ironical eyebrows. Lifting two sheets of foolscap from his desk he said, "You wrote this?"

"Yes sir."

"What gave you the idea?"

"Nothing, sir."

"Hm. I suppose you read a lot?"

"Quite a lot."

"What are you reading just now?"

"A play called *The Dynasts*."

"Hardy's *Dynasts*?"

"I forget who wrote it. I got it out of the library."

"What do you think of it?"

"I think the choruses are a bit boring but I like the scenic directions. I like the retreat from Moscow, with the bodies of the soldiers baked by fire in front and frozen stiff behind. And I like the view of Europe down through the clouds, looking like a sick man with the Alps for his backbone."

"Do you do any writing at home?"

"Oh yes, sir."

"Are you at work on anything just now?"

"Yes. I'm trying to write about this boy who can hear colours."

"Hear colours?"

"Yes sir. When he sees a fire burning each flame makes a noise like a fiddle playing a jig, and some nights he's kept awake by the full moon screaming, and he hears the sun rise through an orange dawn like trumpets blowing. The bother is that most colours round about him make horrible noises— orange and green buses, for instance, traffic lights and advertisements and things."

"You don't hear colours yourself, do you?" said the teacher, looking at Thaw peculiarly.

"Oh no," said Thaw, smiling. "I got the idea from a note Edgar Allan Poe wrote to one of his poems. He said he sometimes thought he could hear the dusk creeping over the land like the tolling of a bell."

"I see. Well, Duncan, the school magazine is rather short of worthwhile contributions this year. Do you think you could write something more for us? Along slightly different lines?"

"Oh yes."

"*Don't* write about the boy who hears colours. It's a good idea—perhaps too good for a school magazine. Write about something more commonplace. How soon could you manage it?"

"Tomorrow, sir."

"The day after will do."

"I'll bring it in tomorrow."

Mr. Meikle tapped his teeth with a pencil end, then said, "We have a debating society in the school every second Wednesday evening. You should come to it. You may have something to say."

Thaw ran leaping back across the empty playground. Outside the maths room he paused, took the grin from his face, frowned with his brows, smiled faintly with his mouth, opened the door and went to his seat with the eyes of the class on him. Kate Caldwell, who sat across the passage from his desk, smiled and flickered questioningly. He bent over a page of axioms, pretending to concentrate but working inwardly on a new story. The elation in his chest recalled the summit of Rua. He remembered the sunlit moor and the beckoning white speck and wondered if these things could be used in a story and if Kate Caldwell would read it and be impressed. Taking a pencil he began to sketch furtively a steep mountain on the cover of a book.

"What is a point?"

He looked up and blinked.

"Stand up, Thaw! Now tell me what a point is."

The question seemed meaningless.

"*A point is that which has no dimensions.* You didn't know that, did you, yet it's the first axiom in the book. And—what's this? You've been drawing on the cover!"

He stared at the teacher's mouth opening and shutting and wondered why the words coming out could hurt like stones. His ear tried to get free by attending to the purr of a car moving slowly up the street outside and the faint shuffle of Kate Caldwell's feet. The teacher's mouth stopped moving. He muttered "Yes miss" and sat down, blushing hotly.

He took four nights to finish the new story properly. He gave it to Mr. Meikle with many apologies for the delay and Mr. Meikle read it and rejected it, explaining that Thaw had tried a blend of realism and fantasy which even an adult would have found difficult. Thaw was stunned and resentful. Though not satisfied with the story he knew it was the best he had written; the words "even an adult" hurt his pride by suggesting his work was only interesting because he was a child; moreover he had quietly told a few classmates of Mr. Meikle's request, hoping word of it would reach Kate Caldwell.

CHAPTER 16. Underworlds

Partly for pleasure, partly to save money, he walked to school each morning through Alexandra Park, mistakenly thinking a twisting path through flowerbeds was shorter than the straight traffic-laden road. The path crossed a hillside with a golf course above and football pitches below. The sky was usually pallid neutral and beyond the pitches a grey pragmatic light illuminated ridges of tenements and factories without obscuring or enriching them. Past the hill a boating pond lay among hawthorn and chestnuts. Often a film of soot had settled overnight on the level water and a duck, newly launched from an island, left a track like the track a finger makes on dusty glass. Crossing the flood of trucks and trams clanging and rumbling on the main road, he picked his way through a grid of small streets by a route which passed two cinemas with still photographs outside and three shops with vividly coloured magazines in the window. The women in these gave his daydreams a more erotic twist.

He had crossed the main road one morning and was descending a short street when Kate Caldwell came out of a close mouth in front of him and walked toward school, her schoolbag (a wartime gas-mask container) bumping at her hip. He followed excitedly, meaning to overtake but lacking the courage. What could he say to her? He imagined his stammering voice saying dull, awkward things about lessons and the weather and could only imagine her saying conventional things in response. Why didn't she turn and smile and beckon? Surely she knew he was behind? If she beckoned he would smile faintly and approach with eyebrows questioningly raised. She would say, "Don't you like my company?" or "I'm glad you come this

way, these morning walks are a bit dull," or "I liked your
story in the school magazine; tell me about yourself." He glared
furiously at her dancing shoulders, willing her to turn and
beckon, but she didn't, and they reached school without getting
nearer together or farther apart. After this he hoped each day
she would come from the close at the exact moment he passed
it so he could speak to her without lowering himself, but either
he didn't see her at all or she emerged ahead and he had to
follow as if towed by an invisible rope. One morning he had
just passed the close when he heard light quick footsteps over-
taking from behind. A confusion of hope and distress hit him,
and a nervous prickling in the skin of his face. Before the
steps reached him he abruptly crossed the road to the opposite
pavement, defiance and self-pity mingling in a sense of tragic
isolation. Then he saw pass him, across the road, not the con-
temptuous dance of Kate Caldwell's shoulderblades but a small,
vigorous old lady with a shopping bag. He reached the playground feeling baffled and disappointed, and afterward went
to school by a route which bothered him with fewer emotional
complications.

Doing well in some subjects, learning to do badly in others
without offending the teachers, he came to accept school as a
sort of bad weather, making only the conventional complaints.
He was friendly with other boys but had no friends and rarely
tried to make them. Apparent life was a succession of dull
habits in which he did what was asked automatically, only resent-
ing demands to show interest. His energy had withdrawn into
imaginary worlds and he had none to waste on reality.

A small fertile land lay hidden in a crater made by an
atomic explosion. Thaw was Prime Minister of it. He lived
in an old mansion among lawns and clumps of forest on the
shore of a loch ornamented with islands. The mansion was
spacious, dim and peaceful. The halls were hung with his paint-
ings, the library full of his novels and poems, there were studios
and laboratories where the best minds of the day worked whenever they cared to visit him. Outside the sun was warm, bees
hummed among flowers and fountains, the season was midway
between summer and autumn when the trees showed their ma-
tured green and only the maples were crimson. Political work
took little of his time, for the people of that country had such
confidence in him that he had only to suggest a reform for it
to be practised. Indeed, his main problem was to keep the

land democratic, for he would have been crowned king long before if his socialist principles had not forbidden it. He looked young for a Prime Minister, being a boy in early adolescence; at the same time he had ruled that land for centuries. He was a survivor of the third world war. The poisonous radiations which had killed most of his contemporaries had, by a fluke, given him eternal youth. In two or three centuries of wandering about the shattered earth he had become leader of a small group of people who had come to trust his gentleness and wisdom. He had brought them to the crater, protected by its walls from the envy of unhappier lands, to build a republic where nobody was sick, poor or forced to live by work they hated. Unluckily his country was surrounded by barbaric lands ruled by queens and tyrants who kept plotting to conquer it and were only kept out by his courage and ingenuity. As a result he was often involved in battles, rescues, escapes, fights with monsters in the middle of arenas, and triumphal processions of shocking vulgarity which he only took part in to avoid hurting the feelings of the queens and princesses whose lives and countries he had saved. When these adventures were over he invited the main characters home to stay with him, and since he annexed the plot of every book and film which impressed him the house by the loch was always crowded with the celebrities of many different races, nations and historical phases. In the simplicity of his spacious rooms they were amazed by the quiet friendliness of a way of life more civilized than their own, and they learned the true duties of a ruler by seeing him spend an afternoon drawing the plans of a new reservoir or university. The women guests usually fell in love with him, though some of the more barbaric came to hate him for his friendly indifference, an indifference which clothed a deep shyness. He could only feel near to women when rescuing them, and often envied the villains who could humiliate or torture them. His position made it impossible to imagine doing such things himself. Yet when walking home from school or public library, these adventures filled his head and chest with such intoxicating emotions that he had to run hard to be relieved of them and often found he had come through several streets without remembering anything of the people, houses or traffic.

His other imaginary world was enjoyed in the genitals. It was a secret gold mine in Arizona which a gang of bandits worked by slave labour. Thaw was bandit chief and spent his time inventing and practising tortures for the slaves. The mine got outside stimulus, not from the shelves of the library but, cryptically, from American comics. He never bought these, and had courage to look at their enticing covers only when the shop contained something else he could pretend to examine, but he sometimes borrowed one at school and in the privacy of the back bedroom copied out pictures of men being whipped and branded. He kept these pictures between pages of Carlyle's *French Revolution*, a book no one else was likely to open.

One evening he knelt by his bed with the pictures on the quilt before him. There was a familiar tension in his genitals but tonight, by a coincidence of positions, his stiffened penis touched a girder upholding the mattress. The contact fired a bolt of white-cold nervous electricity into him in a shock so poignant that he had to press harder and harder against the source of it until something gushed and squirted, the kicking mechanism broke down, shrunk and went limp and he was left feeling horribly flat and emptied out. All the while his mind had sat feebly aghast, wondering what was happening with the slight energy left to it. Now he looked disgustedly at the drawings, took them to the lavatory, flushed them down the pan and opened his trousers.

A grey slug-shaped blob of jelly lay on his stomach just under the navel. It was transparent, tiny milky wisps and galaxies hung in it and it smelled like fish. He wiped himself clean and went back to the bedroom, not knowing what had happened but sure it had to do with the sniggers, hints and sudden silences which instinctive distaste made him ignore among his classmates. He felt numb and disgusted and swore not to think again the thoughts that led to this condition. Two days later they came back and he gave way to them without much resistance.

And now the flow of his imaginative life was broken by three or four orgasms a week. His pleasure in the mine had once lasted indefinitely, for it never reached a climax. After drawing or brooding awhile he would be called to a meal, or to homework, or would go for a walk and return from it the humane triumphant Prime Minister of his republic. Now after brooding on the mine a few minutes his penis would yearn to touch something, and if denied this help often exploded by itself, leaving a sodden stain in his trousers and a self-contempt so great that it included all his imaginary worlds. He was as much estranged from imagination as from reality.

The asthma returned with increasing weight, by day lying on his chest like a stone, at night pouncing like a beast. One night he woke with the beast's paw so hard on his throat that he moved in a moment from fear to utter panic and leaped from bed with a cawing scream, stumbled to the window and clutched back the curtain. A gold flake of moon, a dim wisp of cloud hung above the opposite chimneys. He glared at them like words he could not read and tried to scream again. His father and mother came beside him and gently pressed him back to bed. Mr. Thaw held him tightly while his mother gave an ephedrine pill and brought first hot milk, then hot whisky, and held the cups to his mouth as he drank. His frightened grunting got less. They left him wrapped in a dressing gown, sitting cross-legged against a pile of pillows.

At the height of the panic, while glaring at the irrelevant moon, his one thought had been a certainty that Hell was worse than this. He had not been religiously educated and though he had a tentative faith in God (saying at the end of prayers "If you exist" instead of "Amen") he had none in Hell. Now he saw that Hell was the one truth and pain the one fact which nullified all others. Sufficient health was like thin ice on an infinite sea of pain. Love, work, art, science and law were dangerous games played on the ice; all homes and cities were built on it. The ice was frail. A tiny shrinkage of the bronchial tubes could put him under it and a single split atom could sink a city. All religions existed to justify Hell and all clergymen were ministers of it. How could they walk about with such bland social faces pretending to belong to the surface of life? Their skulls should be furnaces with the fire of Hell burning in them and the skin of their faces dried and thin like scorched leaves. The face of Dr. McPhedron came to him as abruptly as when it was thrust over the edge of the rock. He turned for help to a bookcase beside the bed. It held books got secondhand for sixpence or a shilling, mostly legends and fantasies with some adult fiction and nonfiction. But now the fantasies were imbecile frivolity, and poetry was whistling in the dark, and novels showed life fighting its own agony, and biographies were accounts of struggles toward violent or senile ends, and history was an infinitely diseased worm without head or tail, beginning or end. A shelf held his father's books, works by Lenin and the Webbs, *The History of the Working Classes in Scotland, Humanities Gain from Unbelief, The Harmsworth Encyclo-*

paedia and books about mountaineering. Putting out a desperate hand he took from among these a general history of philosophy, opened at random and read:

All the perceptions of the human mind resolve themselves into two distinct kinds, which I shall call IMPRESSIONS and IDEAS. The difference between these consists of the degrees of force and liveliness with which they strike upon the mind, and make their way into our thought or consciousness. These perceptions, which enter with the most force or violence, we may name *impressions;* and under the name I may comprehend all our sensations, passions and emotions, as they make their first appearance in the soul. By *ideas* I mean the faint image of these in thinking and reasoning. . . .

He read on with increasing relief, brought more and more into a world which, though made of words instead of numbers, was almost mathematical in its cleanness and lack of emotion. Looking up from the book much later he saw between the disordered curtains that the sky was pale and heard a faint distant music, a melodious thrumming which grew louder and louder until it seemed above his head, then faded into the distance. It was too rhythmical for birdsong, too harmonious for aircraft. He was puzzled but oddly comforted and fell into a smooth sleep.

At seven an alarm rang in the living room where his parents slept in the bed settee. Mr. Thaw had breakfast and carried his bicycle downstairs to the street. Mrs. Thaw brought to the bedroom a tray set with porridge, fried egg, sausage, brown bread with marmalade and a cup of tea. She watched as he ate and said, "Is it any better, son?"
"A bit better."
"Ach, you'll be all right when ye get to school."
"Mibby."
"Take another pill."
"I have taken another. It's not doing much good."
"You've made up your mind it's not doing good! If you wanted it to work it *would* work!"
"Mibby."
After a while he said, "Anyway, I don't want to go to school today."
"But, Duncan, the exams are two weeks away."
"I'm tired. I didn't sleep well."
Mrs. Thaw said coldly, "Are you trying to tell me you *can't*

go to school? You weren't very well yesterday but you were well enough to go to the library. You've always enough breath for what you want to do; none for what's important."

Thaw laboriously dressed and washed. Mrs. Thaw helped him on with his coat and said, "Now take your time going down the road. It's church first period so it won't matter if you're a bit late. The teachers understand. And straighten your back. Stop walking about like a half-shut penknife. Look the world in the face as if you owned it."

"I own none of it."

"You own as much of it as anyone! You can own *more* of it if you use your brain and learn to do well in the exams. You have a good brain. Your teachers say so. They want to help you. Why don't you want to be helped?"

There was no special position for praying in. People sat with legs apart or crossed, arms folded, hands clasped or clenched as they pleased, but all shut their eyes to suggest concentration and bowed their heads as a mark of respect. For a long time Thaw had stopped shutting his eyes but lacked the courage to lift his head. Today, arriving late and breathing uneasily, a great carelessness filled him and he impatiently raised his head during a lengthy prayer. He was seated on one side of the gallery with a clear view down on the bent heads of the congregation, the choir, the minister in the octagonal tower of his pulpit and the headmaster at the foot of it. The minister was a fat-faced man whose head wagged and nodded with every phrase while his raptly shut eyes gave it a blind empty look, like a balloon blown about in a draught. Thaw felt suddenly that he was being watched. Among the rows of bowed heads in the gallery opposite was an erect, slightly clumsy, almost expressionless face which, if it noticed him (and he was not sure it did) did so with a faint sarcastic smile. Something in the face made him feel he knew it. Later that day the stranger was introduced into the class as Robert Coulter, who had been promoted to Whitehill Secondary School from Garngad Junior Secondary School. He fitted into the class easily, making friends without effort and doing fairly well at the things Thaw did badly. He and Thaw exchanged embarrassed nods when accident brought them face to face and otherwise ignored each other. Once, in the science room, the pupils stood talking by their benches before the teacher arrived. Coulter approached Thaw and said, "Hullo."

"Hullo."

"How are you getting on?"

"Not too bad. How are you?"

"Ach, not too bad."

After a pause Coulter said, "Would you mind swopping seats?"

"Why?"

"Well, I'd like a closer view. . . ." Coulter pointed at Kate Caldwell. "After all, you're not interested in that sort of thing."

Thaw took his books to Coulter's bench filled with black rage and depression. Nothing could have made him admit his interest in Kate Caldwell.

One day after the exams the teachers sat at their desks correcting papers while the pupils read comics, played chess or cards or talked quietly in groups. Coulter, at a desk in front of Thaw, turned round and said, "What are ye reading?"

Thaw showed a book of critical essays on art and literature. Coulter said accusingly, "You don't read that for fun."

"Yes, I read it for fun."

"People our age don't read that sort of book for fun. They read it to show they're superior."

"But I read this sort of book even when there's nobody to see me."

"That shows you arenae trying to make *us* think you're superior, you're trying to make *yourself* think you're superior."

Thaw scratched his head and said, "That's clever, but not very true. What are you reading?"

Coulter showed him a magazine called *Astounding Science Fiction*, with a picture on the cover of tentacled creatures manipulating a piece of machinery in a jungle clearing. Green lightning leaped from the machine into the sky where it split open a planet which seemed to be the earth. Thaw shook his head and said, "I don't like science fiction much. It's pessimistic."

Coulter grinned and said, "That's what I like about it. I was reading a great story the other day called *Colonel Johnson Does His Duty*. This American colonel is in a hideout miles underground. He's one of those in charge of fighting the third world war, which is all done by pressing switches. Everybody aboveground has been killed, of course, and even a lot of the army folk have had their hideouts blasted by special rockets that bore into the ground. Well, this Colonel Johnson, see, has been out of touch for months with the folks on his own side, because if you use the radio these special rockets can work out where your hideout is and come down and blast you. Anyway, this Colonel Johnson invents a machine that can find out where people are by detecting their thought waves. He starts using the machine on America. No good. Everyone in America's dead. He tries Europe, Africa, Australia. Everybody's dead there too. Then he tries Asia and here there's only one other man left alive in the world, and he's in a city in Russia. So he gets into this plane and flies to Russia. Everything he passes over is dead—no plants or animals or anything. He lands in this Russian city and gets out. Everything's wreckage, of course, but he creeps through it till he hears this other man moving inside this building. It's eight years since he's seen another human being, he's going mad with loneliness, see, and he's been hoping to talk tae another man before he dies. The Russian comes out of the building and Colonel Johnson shoots him."

"But *why?*" said Thaw.

"Because he's been trained tae kill Russians. Don't you like that story?"

"I think it's a rotten story."

"Mibby. But it's true tae life. What do you do after school?"

"I go to the library, or mibby a walk."

"I go intae town with Murdoch Muir and big Sam Lang. We stage riots."

"How?"

"D'ye know the West End Park?"

"The park near the Art Galleries?"

"Aye. Well, they don't lock it up at night like other parks and folk can walk through it. There's a few lights in it but no' many. Well, big Sam'll stand near some bushes and light a fag, and when someone comes we charge out from the bushes and pretend to kick big Sam in the guts and he lashes out with his fists and we all fall down and roll about swearing. We don't touch each other, but in the dark it's hellish convincing. You get lassies running away screaming for the police."

"Don't the police come?"

"We run away before they come. Murdoch Muir's dad is a policeman. When we tell him about it he roars and laughs and tells us whit he would dae tae us if he caught us."

Thaw said, "That's anti-social."

"Mibby, but it's natural. More natural than going walks by yourself. Come on, admit you'd like tae come with us one night."

"But I wouldnae."

"Admit you'd sooner look at that comic than read your art criticism."

Coulter pointed at the cover of a neighbour's comic. It showed

a blonde in a bathing costume being entwined by a huge serpent. Thaw opened his mouth to deny this, then frowned and shut it. Coulter said, "Come on, that picture makes your cock prick, doesn't it? Admit you're like the rest of us."
Thaw went to the next classroom alarmed and confused. "That picture makes your cock prick. Admit you're like the rest of us." He remembered other words heard long before but carefully ignored: "I wouldnae mind feeling *her* belly in a dark room."

He had known from the age of four that babies hatched from their mothers' stomachs. Mr. Thaw had described the growth of the embryo in detail, and Thaw had assumed this process occurred spontaneously in most women above a certain age. He accepted this as he accepted his father's account of the origin of species and the solar system: it was an interesting, mechanical, not very mysterious business which men could know about but not influence. Nothing he heard or read later had mentioned inevitable links between love, sex and birth, so he never thought there were any. Sex was something he had discovered squatting on the bedroom floor. It was so disgusting that it had to be indulged secretly and not mentioned to others. It fed on dreams of cruelty, had its climax in a jet of jelly and left him feeling weak and lonely. It had nothing to do with love. Love was what he felt for Kate Caldwell, a wish to be near her and do things that would make her admire him. He hid this love because public knowledge of it would put him in an inferior position with other people and with Kate herself. He was ashamed of it, but not disgusted. And now, jerkily, under the influence of Coulter's remark, his separate pictures of love, sex and birth started to become one.

He was crossing the hill in the park when he heard musical throbbing come from the sky. Five swans flew over his head in V formation, their thrumming wings and honking throats blending in one music. Lowering their feet they dropped out of sight behind the trees which screened the boating pond. During the next days he collected spare bits of bread and threw them in the pond on his way to school. One morning he saw something that kept him on the shore longer than usual. Beside the island two swans faced each other in such an intent way that he thought they were going to fight. Spreading their wings they rose from the water almost to the tail, pressed their breasts together, then their brows, then their beaks. Pointing their faces skyward they twined necks, then untwisted and coiled them backward, each reflecting the other like a mirror. Together they made and unmade with their bodies the shapes of Greek lyres and renaissance silverware. Suddenly one of them broke the pattern, slipped adroitly behind the other, mounted her tail and thrust his body up and down it while she plunged across the water in a thresh of wings and waves. As they passed Thaw he saw the male push the female's head under water with his beak, perhaps to make her more docile. At the end of the loch they separated, straightened necks and sailed indifferently apart. The female, being more dishevelled, was readjusting her feathers when the male, in a remote bay, started probing unenthusiastically for minnows.

Ten minutes later Thaw joined the lines in the playground full of grey depression. In class he looked coldly on the pupils, the teacher, and Kate Caldwell most of all. They were part of a deceptive surface, horrifying this time not because it was weak and could not keep out Hell but because it was transparent and could not hide the underlying filth. That evening he walked with Coulter along the canal bank and told him about the swans. Coulter said, "Have you seen slugs do it?"
"Slugs?"
"Aye, slugs. When I was on MacTaggart's farm in Kinlochrua I came out one morning after some rain and here were all these slugs lying in the grass in couples. I took them apart and put them together again tae see how they did it. They seemed so human. Much more human than your swans."
Thaw stood still for a moment and then cried aloud, "I wish to God I would never want another human being in my whole life! I wish to God I was . . ."
He paused. A word from a recent botany lesson entered his head. ". . . self-fertilizing! Oh, Lord God Maker and Sustainer of Heaven and Hell make me self-fertilizing! If you exist."
Coulter looked at him, slightly awestruck, then said, "You scare me sometimes, Duncan. The things you say arenae altogether sane. It all comes of wanting to be superior to ordinary life."

CHAPTER 17. The Key

Mr. Thaw worked as a labourer and then as a wages clerk for a firm building housing estates round the city edge. The Korean war began, the cost of living rose and Mrs. Thaw got a job as a shop assistant in the afternoons. She came to feel very tired and suffered depressions which her doctor thought were caused by the change of life. When the tea things had been cleared away in the evenings she would sew or knit, glancing occasionally at Thaw, who sat frowning at the pages of a textbook and fingering his brow or cheek. His inattention drew comments from her.

"You're not working."

"I know."

"You ought to be working. The exams are coming off soon. You've made up your mind not to pass and you won't."

"I know."

"And you could pass if you tried. Your teachers all say you could. And you sit there doing nothing and you'll make us all ashamed of you."

"I'm afraid so."

"Well, do something! And don't scratch! You sit there clot-clot-clotting at your face till it's like a lump of raw meat. Think of your sister Ruth if you won't think of yourself or me. She's ashamed enough as it is of a brother who creeps about the school like a hunchback."

"I can't help my asthma."

"No, but if you did the exercises the physiotherapist at the Royal told you to do you could walk about like a human being. You were told to do five-minutes exercise each morning and evening. How often did you do them? Once."

"Twice."

"Twice. And why? Why don't you want to improve yourself?"
"Laziness, I suppose."
"Hm!"
Thaw pretended once more to study a page of mathematics but found himself brooding on a talk with the head English teacher about the school curriculum. Thaw said much of it was neither interesting in itself nor useful in a practical way. Mr. Meikle had looked thoughtfully across the bent backs and heads of his class and said, "Remember, Duncan, when most people leave school they have to live by work which can't be liked for its own sake and whose practical application is outside their grasp. Unless they learn to work obediently because they're told to, and for no other reason, they'll be unfit for human society."
Thaw sighed, picked up a textbook and read:

> A man and his wife clean their teeth from the same cylindrical tube of toothpaste on alternate days. The interior diameter of the nozzle through which the paste is squeezed is .08 of the interior diameter of the tube, which is 3.4 cms. If the man squeezes out a cylinder of toothpaste 1.82 cms in length each time he uses it, and his wife a cylinder 3.13 cms in length, find the length of the tube to the nearest mm. if it lasts from the 3rd of January to the 8th of March inclusive and the man is the first to use it.

A hysterical rage gripped him. Dropping the book, he clutched at his head and rubbed and scratched and towzled it until his mother shouted "Stop!"
"But this is absurd! This is ludicrous! This is unb-unb-unb-unb-unb-unb"—he choked—"unbearable! I don't understand it, I can't learn it, what good will it do me?"
"It'll get you through your exams! That's all the good it needs to do! You can forget it when you've got your Higher Leaving Certificate!"
"Why can't they examine me in standing on my head balancing chairs on my feet? Homework for that might improve my health."
"And do you really think you know what's good for you better than the teachers and headmasters who've studied the subject all their lives?"
"Yes. Yes. Where my own needs are concerned I do know better."
Mrs. Thaw put a hand to her side and said in a strange voice, "Oh, bloody hell!" Then she said, "Why did I bring

children into the world?" and began weeping.

Thaw was alarmed. It was the first time he had heard her curse or seen her weep and he tried to sound reasonable and calm. "Mummy, it doesnae matter if I fail those exams. If I leave school and get a job you won't need to work so hard."

Mrs. Thaw dabbed her eyes and resumed sewing, her lips pressed tight together. After a pause she said, "And what job will you get? An errand boy's?"

"There must be other jobs."

"Such as?"

"I don't know, but there must be!"

"Hm!"

Thaw shut his books and said, "I'm going for a walk."

"That's right, run away. Men can always run away from work. Women never can."

There was daylight in the sky but none in the streets and the lamps were lit. Boys of his own age strolled on the pavements in crowds of three and four, girls walked in couples, groups of both sexes gossiped and giggled by café doors. Thaw felt inferior and conspicuous. Overheard whispers seemed to mock the absent look he wore to disarm criticism, overheard laughter seemed caused by the upright hair he never brushed or combed. He walked quickly into streets with fewer shops where people moved in enigmatic units. His confidence grew with the darkness. His face took on a resolute, slightly wolfish look, his feet hit the pavement firmly, he strode past couples embracing in close mouths feeling isolated by a stern purpose which put him outside merely human satisfactions. This purpose was hardly one he could have explained (after all he was just walking, not walking to anywhere) but sometimes he thought he was searching for the key.

The key was small and precise, yet in its use completely general and completely particular. Once found it would solve every problem: asthma, homework, shyness before Kate Caldwell, fear of atomic war; the key would make everything painful, useless and wrong become pleasant, harmonious and good. Since he thought of it as something that could be contained in one or two sentences, he had looked for it in the public libraries but seldom on the science or philosophy shelves. The key had to be recognized at once and by heart, not led up to and proved by reasoning. Nor could it be an article of religion, since its discovery would make churches and clergy unnecessary.

Nor was it poetry, for poems were too finished and perfect to finish and perfect anything themselves. The key was so simple and obvious that it had been continually overlooked and was less likely to be a specialist's triumphant conclusion than to be mentioned casually by someone innocent and dull; so he had searched among biographies and autobiographies, correspondences, histories and travel books, in footnotes to outdated medical works and the indexes of Victorian natural histories. Recently he had thought the key more likely to be found on a night walk through the streets, printed on a scrap of paper blown out of the rubble of a bombed factory, or whispered in a dark street by someone leaning suddenly out of a window.

Tonight he came to a piece of waste ground, a hill among tenements that had been suburban twenty years earlier. The black shape of it curved against the lesser blackness of the sky and the yellow spark of a bonfire flickered just under the summit. He left the pallid gaslit street and climbed upward, feeling coarse grass against his shoes and occasional broken bricks. When he reached the fire it had sunk to a few small flames among a heap of charred sticks and rags. He groped on the ground till he found some scraps of cardboard and paper and added them to the fire with a torn-up handful of withered grass. A tall flame shot up and he watched it from outside the brightness it cast. He imagined other people arriving one at a time and standing in a ring round the firelight. When ten or twelve had assembled they would hear a heavy thudding of wings; a black shape would pass overhead and land on the dark hilltop, and the messenger would walk down to them bringing the key. The fire burned out and he turned and looked down on Glasgow. Nothing solid could be seen, only lights— streetlamps like broken necklaces and bracelets of light, neon cinema signs like silver and ruby brooches, the ruby, emerald and amber twinkle of traffic regulators—all glowing like treasure spilled on the blackness.

He went back down to the dingy streets and entered a close in one of the dingiest. The stair was narrow, ill lit and smelling of cat piss. Before a lavatory door on a half landing he stepped over two children who knelt on a rug, playing with a clockwork toy. The top landing had three doors, one with FORBES COULTER on it in Gothic script among gold vine leaves, framed behind glass which the passage of years had blotched

with mildew on the inside. The door was opened by a small woman with an angry cloud of curly grey hair. She said plaintively, "Robert's down in the lavatory Duncan, you'll just have to come in and wait."
Thaw stepped across a cupboard-sized lobby into a tidy comfortable crowded room. Wardrobe, sideboard, table and chairs left narrow spaces between them. A tall window had a sink in front and a gas cooker beside it. A shadow was cast over the fireplace by drying clothes on a pulley in the ceiling, and the table held the remains of a meal.

Mrs. Coulter began moving plates to the sink and Thaw sat by the fire and stared into a bed-recess near the door. Coulter's father lay there, his shoulders supported by pillows, his massive sternly lined blind enduring face turned slightly toward the room.
Thaw said, "Are you any better, Mr. Coulter?"
"In a way, yes, Duncan; but then again, in a way, no. How's the school doing?"
"I'm all right at art and English."
"Art is your subject isn't it? I used to paint a bit myself. During the thirties a few of us—we were unemployed, you know— we got together on Thursday evenings in a room near Brigton Cross and we'd get a teacher or a model along from the art school. We called ourselves the Brigton Socialist Art Club. Have you heard of Ewan Kennedy? The sculptor?"
"I'm not sure, Mr. Coulter. Mibby. I mean the name's familiar but I'm no' sure."
"He was one of us. He went to London and did quite well for himself. A year ago. . . . No. Wait."
Thaw looked at Mr. Coulter's big gnarled hand lying quietly on the quilt, a cigarette with a charred tip between two fingers. "It was three years ago. His name was in the *Bulletin*. He was making a bust of Winston Churchill for some town in England. I thought when I read it, I used to know you."
Mr. Coulter hummed a quiet tune then said, "My father was a picture framer to trade. He did everything in those days, carving the wood, gilding it, even hanging the picture sometimes. Some of his work must be in the Art Galleries to the present day. I used to help him with the hanging. Hanging a picture is an art in itself. What I meant to tell you was this: I was hanging these pictures in a house in Menteith Row on the Green. It's a slum now but the wealthiest folk in Glasgow once lived in those houses, and in my time some of them still

did, and this house belonged to Jardine of Jardine and Beattie, the shipbuilders. Young Jardine was a lawyer and became Lord Provost, and *his* son proved tae be a bit of a rogue, but never mind. I was hanging these pictures in the entrance hall: marble floor, oak-panelled walls. The frames were carved walnut covered with gold leaf, but the hall was dark because there were no windows opening into it, apart from a wee skylight window that was no use at all because it was stained glass. When I had finished I opened the front door and went down the steps onto the pavement outside and stood looking in through the open door. It was a morning in the early spring, cold, but the sun quite bright. A girl came along and said, 'What are ye staring at?' I pointed through the door and said 'Look at that. It looks like a million dollars.' The sun was shining intae the hall and the gold frames were shining on the walls. It really did look like a million dollars.''

Mr. Coulter smiled a little.

Coulter entered and said, "Hullo, Duncan. Hullo, Forbes. Forbes, your cigarette's out. Will I light it for you?"

"Ye can light it if you like."

Coulter got a match and lit the cigarette, then went to the sink, put an arm round his mother's waist, and said, "My ain wee mammy, how about a fag? You've given my daddy a fag, give me a fag."

Mrs. Coulter took a cigarette packet from her apron pocket and handed it over, grumbling, "You're no' old enough tae smoke but."

"True, but my wee mammy can refuse me nothing. Have these two been discussing art?"

"Aye, they've been talking about their art."

"Well, Thaw, my intellectual friend, what's it to be? A game of chess or a dauner along the canal bank?"

"I wouldnae mind a dauner."

They walked on the towpath talking about women. Coulter had dropped the hard cheerful manner he wore at home. Thaw said, "The only time I reach them is when I speak at the debating society. Even Kate Caldwell notices me then. She was in the front row of desks last night, staring at my face with her mouth and eyes wide open. I felt dead witty and intellectual. I felt like a king or something. She sits behind me at maths now. I've made a poem about it."

He paused, hoping that Coulter would ask him to recite. Coulter said, "Everybody writes poems about girls at our age. It's what they call a phase. Even big Sam Lang writes poems about girls. Even I occasionally—"

"Never mind. I like my wee poem. Bob, if I ask you a question will ye promise to answer truthfully?"

"Ask away."

"Is Kate Caldwell keen on me?"

"Her? On you? No."

"I think she's mibby a bit keen on me."

"She's a wee grope," said Coulter.

"What?"

"A grope. A feel. Lyle Craig in the fifth year is supposed to be winching her steady, and last Friday I saw her being lumbered by a hardman up a close near the Denistoun Palais."

"Lumbered?"

"Groped. Felt. She's nothing but a wee—"

"Don't use that word!" cried Thaw.

They walked in silence until at last Coulter said, "I shouldnae have told you that, Duncan."

"But I'm glad. Thank you."

"I'm sorry I told you."

"I'm not. I want to know every obstacle, every obstacle there is. There's the obstacles of not being attractive, not having money to take her out, not knowing how to talk to her, and now it seems she's a flirt. If I ever reach her she'll shift elsewhere and keep on shifting."

"Mibby it's a mistake to start with Kate Caldwell. You should practise on someone else first. Practise on my girl, big June Haig."

"Your girl?"

"Well, I've only been out with her once. There's a big demand for her."

"What's she like?"

"She's got a back like an all-in wrestler. Her arms are as thick as my thighs and her thighs as thick as your waist. Cuddling her is like sinking intae a big sofa."

"You hardly make her sound attractive."

"Big June is the most attractive girl I know. She's exciting and she's comfortable. Ask her to the third-year dance."

Thaw remembered June Haig. She was a sulky-looking girl and not as large as Coulter pretended, but she had failed to get out of the second year and was called Big June to distinguish her from the less developed girls she sat among. Thaw felt a pang of interest. He said, "Big June wouldnae come to a dance with me."

"She might. She doesnae like you but she's intrigued by your reputation."

"Have I a reputation?"

"You've two reputations. Some say you're an absentminded professor with no sex life at all; others say that's just a disguise and you've the dirtiest sex life in the whole school."

Thaw stood still and held his head. He cried, "I see no way out, no way out. I want to be close to Kate, I want to be valued by her, I suppose I want to marry her. What bloody good is this useless wanting, wanting, wanting?"

"Don't think your problems would be solved by marrying her."

"Why not?"

"Fornication isnae just sticking it in and wagging it around. You've tae time things so that when you're pushing hardest she's exactly ready to take it. If ye don't get this exactly right she feels angry and disappointed with you. It needs a lot of practice tae get right."

"Examinations!" cried Thaw. "It's all examinations! Must everything we do satisfy someone *else* before it's worthwhile? Is everything we do because we enjoy it selfish and useless? Primary school, secondary school, university, they've got the first twenty-four years of our lives numbered off for us and to get into the year above we've to pass an exam. Everything is done to please the examiner, never for fun. The one pleasure they allow is anticipation: 'Things will be better after the exam.' It's a lie. Things are never better after the exam. You'd think love was something different. Oh, no. It has to be studied, practised, learnt, and you can get it wrong."

"You're eloquent tonight," said Coulter. "You've got me almost as mixed up as yourself. But not quite. You see there's really no connection between—"

"*What's that?*"

"That? A kid singing."

They were beside a fence of old railway sleepers planted upright at the towpath edge. From the other side a clear tuneless little voice sang:

> "Ah've a laddie in Ame-e-e-rica,
> Ah've a laddie ower the sea;
> Ah've a laddie in Ame-e-e-rica,
> And he's goantae marry me."

They looked through a gap in the sleepers onto a road with the canal embankment on one side and the black barred windows of a warehouse on the other. A small girl was skipping with a rope and singing to herself in a circle of light under a lamp. Coulter said, "That kid's too young to be up at this hour. What are ye grinning at?"

"I thought for a moment her words might be the key."

"What key?"

Thaw explained about the key, expecting it would send Coulter into a fit of annoyance, as most of his less practical concepts did. Coulter frowned and said, "Has this key to be words?"

"What else could it be?"

"When I was staying with auld MacTaggart in Kinlochrua during the war I remember two or three nights when I got a good view of the stars. Ye can always see more stars when you're in the country, especially if there's a nip of frost in the air, and these nights the sky was just hotching with stars. I felt this . . . this coming nearer and nearer me till I almost had it, but when I tried tae think what it was, it had gone. And this happened more than once."

"I don't know what you mean. What sort of thing was it? Did it tie up everything you believed? Could ye test things with it?"

"You could test nothing with it. It was a feeling, I suppose. It was gentle, and permanent, and more like a friend than anything else."

Thaw was unable to think of a similar experience and felt envious. He said, "It sounds a bit sentimental. Did you only feel it when you were seeing stars?"

"That was the only time."

Thaw looked at the sky. Though at first sight it was merely dark his eyes gradually resolved it into brownish-purple, turning dull orange on the horizon toward the city centre. Thaw said, "Why is it that colour?"

"I suppose it's the electric light reflected back from the gas and soot in the air."

They reached a point halfway between their homes and said goodbye. After Thaw had gone forward a few yards by himself he heard a cry from behind. He turned and saw Coulter wave and shout, "Don't worry! Don't worry! Tae hell with Kate Caldwell!"

Thaw walked onward with a small perfect image of Kate Caldwell smiling and beckoning inside him. Such a fog of desperate emotions was wrapped round it that at last he had to halt and gasp for breath. On the far bank of the canal stood the vast sheds of the Blochairn ironworks. Dull bangs and clangs came from these, an orange glare flickered on the sky above them, the canal water bubbled blackly and wisps of steam waltzed on the surface and flew in a cloud over the towpath. A high railing divided the path from the Alexandra park. Taking a great breath he rushed at this, gripped two spikes on top, pulled himself up and jumped down onto the golf course. He ran along the fairways feeling exalted and criminal and came to a place where trees grew from smooth turf around the pagoda of an ornamental fountain. The grey lawns with dim galaxies of daisies on them, the silhouettes of the trees and fountain, were excitingly unlike themselves as he had seen them on the way from school a few hours before. Stepping over a "Keep Off the Grass" sign he went to a tree he had often wished to climb. It had no branches for the first twelve feet but it was craggy and crooked and he climbed high into it before the impetus which had driven him over the railing ran out and left him astride a high bough with his arms round the trunk. He recalled Greek stories about female spirits who lived inside trees. It was possible to imagine that the trunk between his arms contained the body of a woman. He hugged it, pressed his face against it and whispered, "I'm here. I'm here. Will you come out?" He imagined the woman's body pressing the other side of the bark, her lips wrestling to meet his lips, but he felt nothing but roughness so he let go and climbed higher until the branches swung under his feet. Overhead the purple-brown sky had been pricked by a star or two. He tried to feel something gentle, permanent and friendly in them until he felt absurd, then climbed down and went home.

Mrs. Thaw opened the door to him. She said, "Duncan, how did you get in that mess?"
"What mess?"
"Your face is pot black, pot black all over!"
He went to the bathroom and looked in the mirror. His face was smeared with sooty grime, especially round the mouth.

CHAPTER 18. Nature

The manageress of the Kinlochrua Hotel was a friend of Mrs. Thaw and invited her children north for the summer holidays. They boarded a bus one morning in a garage on the Broomielaw and it took them through shadows of warehouses and tenements into bright sunlight on the broad, tree-lined Great Western Road. They hurled past Victorian terraces and gardens and hotels, past merchants' villas and municipal housing schemes into a region which (though open to the sky) could not be called country. New factories stood among tracts of weed and thistle, pylons grouped on hillsides and wire fences protected rows of grassy domes joined by metal tubes. The Clyde on their left widened to a firth, the central channel marked by buoys and tiny lighthouses. A long oil tanker moved processionally seaward between tugboats and was passed by a cargo ship going the other way. The hills on the right got steeper and nearer, the road was pinched between the river and a wooded crag, then they saw ahead of them the great rock of Dumbarton upholding the ancient fort above the roofs of the town. The bus turned north up the Vale of Leven, sometimes travelling between fields and sometimes through the crooked streets of industrial villages, then it reached the broad glittering water of Loch Lomond and ran along the western shore. Islands lay with trees, fields and cottages on them like broken-off pieces of the surrounding land, and on the far side arose the great head and shoulders of Ben Lomond. Fields gave way to heather and the islands grew small and rocky. The Loch became a corridor of water between high-sided bens, with the road twisting through trees and boulders at the feet of them.

The bus was full of folk going north for the holidays. Climbers sat at the back singing bawdy mountaineering songs and Thaw pressed his brow to the cool window and felt desperate. On leaving home he had taken a grain of effedrine and boarded the bus feeling fairly well, but beyond Dumbarton his breathing worsened and now he tried to forget it by concentrating on the ache the vibrating glass made in the bones of his skull. In the passing land outside the colours were raw green or dead grey: grey road, crags and tree trunks, green leaves, grass, bracken and heather. His eyes were sick of dead grey and raw green. The yellow or purple spots of occasional roadside flowers shrieked like tiny discords in an orchestra where every instrument played over and over again the same two notes. Ruth said, "Feeling cheesed off, brother mine?"

"A bit. It's getting worse."

"Cheer up! You'll be fine when we arrive."

"It's not easy."

"Ach, you're too pessimistic. I'm sure you wouldnae get so bad if you were less pessimistic."

The bus stopped on a hillside in Glencoe to let climbers off and the passengers were told they could stretch their legs for five minutes. Thaw got laboriously out and sat on a sun-warmed bank of turf at the roadside. Ruth stood with climbers taking their rucksacks from the boot and talked to someone she had met when climbing with her father. The other passengers gossiped and glanced at the surrounding peaks with expressions of satisfaction or puzzled resentment. An elderly man said to his neighbour, "Aye, a remarkable vista, a remarkable vista."

"You're right. If these stones could talk they would tell us some stories, eh? I bet they could tell us some stories."

"Aye, from scenes like these Auld Scotia's grandeur springs." Thaw looked upward and saw huge chunks of raw material hacked about by time and weather. From cracks in the highest a rocky rubble spilled over heathery slopes like stuff poured down slag-bings. A boy and girl in shorts and climbing boots strode past him down the road, the boy with a small rucksack bumping between his shoulders. The climbers by the bus cheered and whistled after them: they joined hands and grinned without embarrassment. The assurance of the boy, the ordinary beauty of the girl, the happy ease of both struck a pang of rage and envy into Thaw which almost made him choke. He glared at a granite slab on the turf beside him. It carried patches of lichen the shape, colour and thickness of scabs he had scratched from his thigh the night before. He imagined the lichen's microscopic roots poking into imperceptible pores in what seemed a solid surface, making them wider and deeper. 'A disease of the rock,' he thought, 'A disease of matter like the rest of us.'

Back in the bus Ruth said, "That was Harry Logan and Sheila. They're going to do the Buchail and spend the night in Cameron's bothy. I wouldnae mind being Sheila for today. Not for tonight, but for today." She laughed and said, "Are you very bad, Duncan? Why not take another pill?"
"I've done that."
Ten minutes later he knew the asthma had grown too strong for pills and he began fighting it with his only other weapon. Withdrawing to the centre of his mind he recalled images from bookshop windows and American comics: a nearly naked blonde smiling as if her body was a joke she wanted to share, a cowering dishevelled girl with eyes and mouth apprehensively open, a big-breasted woman with legs astride and hands on hips and a sullen selfish stare which seemed to invite the most selfish kind of assault. His penis stiffened and he breathed easily. He fixed on the last of these women and her face became the face of big June Haig. He imagined meeting her in the precipitous waste landscapes through which the bus was rushing. She wore white shorts and shirt but high-heeled shoes instead of climbing boots, and he raped her at great length with complicated mental and physical humiliations. To stop these thoughts from coming to a climax of masturbation he sometimes wrenched his mind from them and sat amazed that thought could make such strong bodily changes. As his penis shrank the asthma got hard and heavy in chest and throat; then his mind gripped the image of the woman once more and a tingling chemical excitement spread again through his blood, widening all its channels and swelling the penis below and the air passages above. And behind it all suffocation waited like an unfulfilled threat.

The bus stopped in a street of uninteresting houses on the shore of a loch. Thaw and Ruth got out and found their mother's friend awaiting them in a car. Ruth sat in front beside her. She was a small lady with a tight mouth and an abrupt way with the gear lever. Thaw, dumb with sexual broodings, sat in the back seat hardly listening to the conversation.
"Is Mary still working in that drapery?"
"Yes, Miss Maclaglan."

"A pity. A pity your father can't get a better job. Won't these open-air organizations he does so much for *pay* him anything?"
"I don't think so. He only works for them in his spare time."
"Hm. Well, I hope you're very helpful to your mother around the house. She isn't at all well, you know."
Ruth and Thaw gazed out of the window in embarrassment. The road undulated in slanting sunlight over a great boggy moor with small irregular lochans in the folds of it. The summit of a conical peak arose beyond the curve of the moor's horizon, and Thaw saw, with distaste, it was Ben Rua. To keep sexually excited he had been forced to imagine increasingly perverse things and now whatever in the outer world recalled other experiences upset him by its irrelevance. They came to the height of the moor and descended toward an arm of the sea with Kinlochrua on the other side, a strip of cottage-flecked lands beneath a grey and grey-green mountain. The tide was out and the clear shallow brine, reflecting blue sky over yellow sands, made a colour like emeralds. A sudden muffled clattering hurt their eardrums. Miss Maclaglan said, "They're testing something at the munition factory. Let's hope it isn't atomic."
"Wasn't the munition factory shut down when the war stopped?" said Ruth.
"Yes, it was shut for almost a year; then the Admiralty took it over. They've taken over the hostel too but they haven't opened it yet, more's the pity. The hostel was the best thing that ever happened here, it shook up their ideas a bit. Kinlochrua was dead before and it's been dead since. Do you know that Mary Thaw is the only real friend I've made in the place? How can you be friendly with women who're afraid to knit on Sundays because of what the minister will say? What has nosey old McPhedron to do with their knitting? Your brother isn't too well, is he?"
Ruth turned and gave Thaw a glance which meant, Pull yourself together. She said, "He's having one of his wheezy spells, but he's got pills for it."
"Well, I think he should go straight to bed the moment we get to the hotel."

At the hotel Miss Maclaglan showed him upstairs to a small clean flower-patterned bedroom. He undressed slowly, removing a shoe and staring for ten minutes through the window, postponing from moment to moment the effort of removing the next. Outside lay a mossy ill-kept garden hidden by a wing of the building from the well-kept gardens in front. It was

hemmed in by dark green cypresses and pines. Small paths
and hedges were arranged round a square half-stagnant pond
with a broken sundial in the middle. The whole place fascinated
him with a sense of sluggish malignant life. The hedges were
half withered by the grasses pushing up among them; the grasses
grew lank and unhealthy in the shadows of the hedges. With
more fibrous limbs than the millipede has legs various plants
struggled in the poor soil, fighting with blind deliberation to
suffocate or strangle each other. Between the roots moved in-
sects, maggots and tiny crustaceans: jointed things with stings
and pincers, soft pursy things with hard voracious mouths, hard-
backed leggy things with multiple eyes and feelers, all gnawing
holes and laying eggs and squirting poisons in the plants and
each other. In the corruption of the garden he sensed something
friendly to his own malign fantasies. Convulsively, he wrenched
off the other shoe, undressed and got into bed. Miss Maclaglan
brought in a hot-water bottle and asked if he would like anything to read. He said no, he had his own books. Ruth brought
up a meal on a tray. He ate, then lay and masturbated. Ten
minutes later he masturbated again. After that he had no weap-
ons to use against the asthma at all.

The garden behind the hotel was overlooked by a dusty
porch containing a massive table and some chairs too worn
for use inside. Next day he sat there with books and painting
tools. Breathing heavily, he made pencil drawings, emphasized
the best ones with India ink and tinted the result with watercolours. While he worked the asthma came to bother him less,
and as he had hardly slept the night before he shut his eyes,
leaned over the table and rested his brow upon clenched fists.
He could hear the air lightly stirring the branches of the trees,
the infrequent call of a bird and a wasp buzzing in the corner
of the porch, but he listened most intently to a murmuring
in his own head, a vague remote sound like the conversation
of two people in an adjacent room. One speaker was excited
and raised his voice so much above the steady drone of the
other that Thaw almost heard the words: ". . . ferns and grass
what's wonderful about grass . . ."

An external sound made him look up. The minister stood
on the sunlit path beyond the shadow of the porch watching
him in an interested way. His buttoned-up black figure was
as Thaw remembered, but smaller, and the face more kindly.
He said, "They tell me you are not well."

"I'm a lot better this morning, thanks."

The minister stepped into the porch and looked at a drawing. "And who is this fellow?"

"Moses on Sinai."

"What a wild wee man he looks among all that rock and thunder. So you are illustrating the bible."

Thaw spoke tonelessly to keep the note of pride out of his voice. "No. I'm illustrating a lecture I'm to give to the school debating society. It's called 'A Personal View of History.' The pictures will be enlarged onto a screen by epedaiescope."

"And what place has Moses in your view of history?"

"He's the first lawyer."

The minister laughed and said, "In a sense, yes, no doubt, Duncan; but then again, in a sense, no. What's this you are reading?" He picked up a thin book with a glossy cover.

"Professor Hoyle's lectures on continuous creation."

The minister sat down on a chair with his hands on the umbrella handle and his chin resting on his hands. "And what does Professor Hoyle tell us about the creation?"

"Well, most astronomers think all the material in the universe was once compressed in a single gigantic atom, which exploded, and all the stars and galaxies in the universe are bits of that old atom. You know that all the galaxies in the universe are rushing away from each other, don't you?"

"I have heard rumours to that effect."

"It's more than rumour, Dr. McPhedron, it's proved fact. Well, Professor Hoyle thinks all the material of the universe is made out of hydrogen, because the hydrogen atom is the simplest form of atom, and he thinks hydrogen atoms are continually coming into existence in the increasing spaces between the stars and forming new stars and galaxies and things."

"Dear me, is that not miraculous! And you believe it?"

"Well, it isn't definitely proved yet, but I like it better than the other theory. It's more optimistic."

"Why?"

"Well, if the first theory is true then one day the stars will burn out and the universe will be nothing but empty space and cold black lumps of rock. But if Professor Hoyle is right there will always be new stars to replace the dead ones."

The minister said politely, "I am fortunate to be rescued from a dying universe at the moment of finding myself menaced by it."

When Thaw had worked out what the minister meant he felt oppressed and angry. He said "Dr. McPhedron, you talk and—

and smile as if everything I say is stupid. What do you believe
in that makes you superior? Is it God?"

The minister said gravely, "I believe in God."

"And that he's good? And made everything? And loves what
he made?"

"I believe those things too."

"Well, why did he make baby cuckoos so that they can only
live by killing baby thrushes? Where's the love in that? Why
did he make beasts that can only live by killing other beasts?
Why did he give us appetites that we can only satisfy by hurting
each other?"

The minister grinned and said, "Dear me. God himself might
be afraid to sit an examination like this. However, I'll do my
best. You talk, Duncan, as if I believed that the world as it is
is the work of God. That is not true. The world was made
by God, and made beautiful. God gave it to man to look after
and keep beautiful, and man gave it to the Devil. Since then
the world has been the Devil's province, and an annexe of
Hell, and everyone born into it is damned. We have either
to earn our bread by the sweat of our brow or steal it from
our neighbours. In either case we live in a state of anxiety,
and the more intelligent we are the more we feel our damnation
and the more anxious we become. You, Duncan, are intelligent.
Mibby you've been searching the world for a sign of God's
existence. If so, you have found nothing but evidence of his
absence, or less, for the spirit ruling the material world is callous
and malignant. The only proof that our Creator is good lies
in our dissatisfaction with the world (for if the God of nature
had made us the life of nature would suit us) and in the works
and words of Jesus Christ, someone you may have read of.
Has Christ a place in your view of history?"

"Yes," said Thaw boldly. "I regard him as the first man to
make a religion of the equal worth of each individual."

"I'm glad you present him as something so respectable, but
he's more than that. He is the way, the truth and the life. To
find God you must believe Christ *was* God and discard every
other knowledge as useless and vain. Then you must pray for
grace."

Thaw shifted several times uncomfortably during this speech,
for it embarrassed him; also, he was finding it hard to keep
his eyes open. After a half minute of silence he realized a question was expected and said, "What's grace?"

"The Kingdom of Heaven in your own heart. The sure knowledge that you are no longer damned. Freedom from anxiety.

God does not send it to all believers, and to few believers
for very long."

"Do you mean that even if I become a Christian I can never
be sure of . . . of . . ."

"Salvation. Dear me, no. God is not a reasonable man like
your grocer or bank manager, giving an ounce of salvation
for an ounce of belief. You can't bargain with him. He offers
no guarantee. I see I am boring you, Duncan, and I'm sorry
for it, though I've said nothing that almost every Scotsman
did not take for granted from the time of John Knox till two
or three generations back, when folk started believing the world
could be improved."

Thaw held his head between his hands feeling depressed and
dull. The minister's answer was more thorough than he had
expected and he felt trapped by it. Though certain there were
many sound counter arguments, the only one he could think
of was "What about the cuckoos?"

The minister looked puzzled.

"Why did God make cuckoos so that they have to live by
killing thrushes? Did they give the world to the Devil too?
Or did the thrushes?"

The minister got up and said, "The life of brute beasts, Duncan,
is so different from ours that strong feelings for them are bound
to be vanity and self-deception. Even your father the atheist
would agree with me in that. I understand you will be here
a week or two. Mibby we can discuss these matters another
time. Meanwhile, I hope you have better health."

"Thank you," said Thaw. He pretended to scribble on a piece
of paper till the minister had gone then folded his arms on
the edge of the table and laid his head on them. He was very
tired but if he lost consciousness for a moment the beast of
suffocation might pounce on his chest, so he tried to rest without
actually sleeping. This was difficult. He got up, collected his
things and went slowly to bed.

That afternoon his memory of what is was like to be well
faded and hope of improvement faded with it. The only imagin-
able future was a repetition of a present which had shrunk to
a tiny painful act, a painful breath drawn again and again from
an ocean of breath. No longer companioning erotic fancies
(which, like the pills, had got useless through overuse) the
sluggish resolute life of the garden grated on him as it grated
on the soil feeding it. He felt the natural world stretching
out from each wall of the hotel in great tracts of lumpy earth

and rock coated thickly with *life,* a stuff whose parts renewed themselves by eating each other. Two or three hundred miles to the south was a groove in the earth with a gathering of stone and metal in it—Glasgow. In Glasgow he had been aided a little by a feeling that among many people someone might hear and help if he screamed loudly enough. But among these mountains screaming was useless; his pain was as irrelevant as the pain of the thrush starved out by the cuckoo, the snail crushed by the thrush. He started screaming but stopped at once. He tried to think but his thoughts were trapped by the minister's speech. How could the world be justified except as punishment? Punishment for what?

That evening Miss Maclaglan phoned for a doctor. He entered Thaw's room and sat by the bed, a not quite middle-aged man in plus fours with a black moustache and squarish head sunk so far into his shoulders that he seemed unable to move it independently of his body. He took Thaw's pulse and temperature, asked how long he had been like this and grunted sombrely. Miss Maclaglan brought a pan of boiling water with a small metal cage clipped inside it. He took glass and metal parts from the cage, fitted them together into a hypodermic syringe, filled this from a rubber-capped bottle then asked Thaw to pull up his pyjama sleeve. Thaw stared at a corner of the ceiling, trying to think of nothing but a crack in it. He felt the muscle of his upper arm wiped with something cold and then the needle running in. The steel point breaking through layers of tissue set his teeth on edge. There was a faint ache as the muscle swelled with pumped-in fluid, then the needle was withdrawn and an amazing thing started to happen. There spread through his body from the arm, but this time unsustained by thought, the tingling liberating flood he had only been able to make erotically. Each nerve, muscle, joint and limb relaxed, his lungs expanded with sufficient air, he sneezed twice and lay back feeling altogether comfortable and well. There was no sense of asthma waiting to return. He could not believe he would ever be unwell again. He looked out into the sun-warm garden. An overgrown rosebush beside the pond had put out white blossoms, and the black dot of a bee moved over one. Surely the bee was enjoying itself? Surely the bush grew because it liked to grow? Everything in the garden seemed to have grown to its appropriate height and now rested a moment, preserved in the amber light of the evening sun. The garden looked *healthy.* Thaw turned with servile gratitude to the ordinary depressed-looking man who had made this change in things. The doctor was examining books and drawings on the bedside table and frowning slightly. He said, "Any better?"

"Yes, thanks. Thanks a lot. I'm a lot better. I can sleep now."

"Mm. I suppose you know that your kind of asthma is partly a psychological illness."

"Yes."

"You do a lot of reading, don't you?"

"Yes."

"Do you abuse yourself?"

"Certainly, if I've been stupid in public."

"No no. I mean, do you masturbate?"

Thaw's face went red. He stared down at the quilt.

"Yes."

"How often?"

"Four or five times a week."

"Mm. That's quite often. It's not widely agreed upon yet, but there is evidence that nervous diseases are aggravated by masturbation. The inmates of lunatic asylums, for instance, masturbate very often indeed. I would try to cut it out if I were you."

"Yes. Yes, I will."

"Here's a bottle of isoprenaline tablets. If you get bad again, break one in two and let half dissolve under your tongue. I think you'll find it'll help."

Thaw was left feeling faintly worried, but fell asleep almost at once.

He woke late at night and worse than ever. The isoprenaline tablets had no effect and the image of June Haig occurred to him, potent and burning like a hot poker in the blood of his stomach. He thought, 'If only I think things about her it will be all right. I don't need to masturbate.' He thought things about her and masturbated ten minutes later. The beast of suffocation pounced at once. He clenched his fists against his chest and dragged breath into it with a gargling sound. Fear became panic and broke his mind into a string of gibbering half-thoughts that would not form: I can't you are I won't it does it will drowning no no no no drowning in no no no no air I can't you are it does. . . .

A thundering hum filled his brain. He was about to faint when a sudden thought formed complete—*If I deserve this it is good*—and around the thought his mind began exultingly to reassemble. He grinned into the bulb of the bedside lamp. He was in pain, but not afraid. Breathing hoarsely, he took a notebook and pen from the bedside table and wrote in big shapeless words:

> *Lord God you exist you exist my punishment proves it. My punishment is not more than I can bear what I suffer is just already the pain is less because I know it is just I won't ever do that thing again, it will be a hard fight but with your help I am able for it I won't ever do that thing again.*

Next day he did it three times. Miss Maclaglan sent a telegram to his mother, who came north by bus the day after. She stood by the bed and smiled sadly down at him. "So you're not too well, son."

He smiled back.

"Ach," she said, "You're a poor auld man. Get a bit better and I'll stay on with you awhile. It'll be an excuse for me to have a holiday too."

He was moved to a big low-ceilinged room with two beds in it. One was his, and Ruth and his mother shared the other. That night when the lights were out Ruth said, "Sing to us, Mummy. It's a long time since you sang to us."

Mrs. Thaw sang some lullabies and sentimental lowland songs: *Ca' the Yowes, Hush-a-baw Birdie, This is No' My Plaid.* She had once won certificates at musical festivals with her singing, but now she only managed the high notes by singing them very softly, almost in a whisper. She tried to sing *Bonnie George Campbell,* which starts with a loud wild lamenting note, but her voice cracked and went tuneless and she stopped and laughed: "Ach, it's beyond me now. I'm getting an auld woman."

"No! you're not!" Thaw and Ruth shouted together. Her words alarmed them. She said, "I think we should try to sleep."

He lay against his pillows breathing heavily. When he coughed Mrs. Thaw said hopefully, "That's right son, bring it up," and afterward, "There now, that's better, isn't it?"

But he had brought up hardly anything, and nothing was better, and the sense of her lying awake attending to the pains in his chest made them harder to bear. He tried to be as still as possible, keeping the small lumps in his gullet until the silence from the other bed made him think she was asleep, but as soon as he coughed, however stealthily, the creak of a mattress told him she was awake and listening.

Suddenly he was sitting up and laughing in the darkness. He had been thinking about the key, or perhaps dreaming of it, and now he saw the universe and the meaning of things. It was hard to put his vision into words but he wanted to share it. "Everything is hate," he gabbled dreamily. "We are all hate, big balloons of hate. Tied together by Ruth's hair ribbons."

The two women screamed. Mrs. Thaw said in a high-pitched voice, "That settles it. We're going back. We're going back tomorrow. There must be *somebody* who knows how to cure him."

Ruth yelled, "You're selfish, utterly selfish! You just don't care about anyone but yourself!" and started crying. Thaw felt puzzled, knowing the words had not conveyed what he meant to convey. He tried again.

"Men are pies that bake and eat themselves, and the recipe is hate. I seem to be buried in this rockery . . ." for though he could dimly see the bedroom, and knew where his mother and sister lay, he also felt buried up to the armpits in a heap of earth and rocks. Mrs. Thaw shouted, "Shut up! Shut up!"

Next morning Thaw and his mother returned to Glasgow. Ruth was allowed to stay behind. That day a boat called at Kinlochrua and Miss Maclaglan drove them to the pier and waved from it as they put to sea. The sun shone as bright as when he had arrived five days before, and for the first time since arriving he saw the great green side of Ben Rua. A clean hard wind was blowing. A member of the crew, a thin boy of Thaw's age, leaned against the funnel playing a concertina. Gulls with spread wings hung above in the rushing air. Thaw sat on a ventilator which stuck out of the deck like an aluminium toadstool, and nearby his mother waved to the figure on the receding pier. On the mountaintop he could make out the white dot of the triangulation point. He thought of the previous night and tried to recover from the muddle of darkness and crying his vision of the key. He seemed to have thought that, just as hydrogen was the basic stuff of the universe, so hatred was the basic material of the mind. In the fresh sunlight it was not a convincing idea. He felt amazingly weak, yet liberated, and while sitting still was not conscious of asthma at all.

Two days later Thaw walked jauntily into town with Coulter to visit the Art Galleries. He talked about the visit to Kinlochrua and what the doctor said. Coulter became angry. "That's daft!" he said. "Everybody masturbates at our age. It's natural. We produce the stuff; how else can we get rid of it? Five times a week sounds about normal to me."

"But that doctor said that in lunatic asylums they do it all the time."

"I believe him. Lunatics are like us. They arenae allowed to have sex in other ways. And what else can they do with their time?"

"But whenever I do it nowadays I have another attack."

"I can believe it. That doctor made you think you would have asthma when you masturbate so you have asthma. Anybody can make you believe anything if they try hard enough. I remember once making you think I was a German spy."

Thaw started grinning. "The funny thing is," he said, "that doctor had me believing in God as well."

"How? No, don't tell me, I see how," said Coulter with disgust, "I bet you felt very special and superior, being punished by God for something he doesnae give a damn for in other folk. Well, I hate to disappoint you, but ye may as well leave God and masturbation out of it and go back to having asthma in the normal way."

CHAPTER 19.
Mrs. Thaw Disappears

Thaw opened his diary and wrote:

"Love seeketh not itself to please Nor for itself hath any care But for another gives its ease and builds a Heaven in Hell's despair." So sung a little Clod of Clay trodden by the cattle's feet, but a Pebble of the brook warbled out these metres meet. "Love seeketh only Self to please, to bind another to Its delight, Joys in another's loss of ease, and builds a Hell in Heaven's despite."

Blake doesn't choose, he shows both sorts of love, and life would be easy if women were clods and men were pebbles. Maybe most of them are but I'm a gravelly mixture. My pebble feelings are all for June Haig, no, not real June Haig, an imaginary June Haig in a world without sympathy or conscience. My feelings for Kate Caldwell are cloddish, I want to please and delight her, I want her to think me clever and fascinating. I love her in such a servile way that I'm afraid to go near her. This afternoon Mum was operated on for something to do with her liver. It seems that for the past year or two old Doctor Poole has been treating her for the wrong illness. I'm ashamed to notice that yesterday I forgot to record that she'd been taken into hospital. I must be a very cold selfish kind of person. If Mum died I honestly don't think I'd feel much about it. I can't think of anyone, Dad, Ruth, Robert Coulter, whose death would much upset or change me. Yet when reading a poem by Poe last week, Thou wast that all to me, love, for which my soul did pine, etc., I felt a very poignant strong sense of loss and wept six tears, four with the left eye, two with the right. Mum isn't going to die of course but this coldness of mine is a bit alarming.

They entered a vast ward in the Royal Infirmary flooded, through tall windows, with grey light from the sky outside. Mrs. Thaw leaned on her pillows looking sick and gaunt yet oddly young. Many lines of strain had been washed from her face by the anaesthetic. She looked more mournful than usual but less worried. Thaw got behind the bed and carefully combed the hair which lay matted around her head and neck. He took a strand at a time in his left hand and combed with the right, noticing how its darkness had been given a dusty look by the grey threads in it. He could think of nothing to say and the combing gave a feeling of closeness without the strain of words. Mr. Thaw said, holding his wife's hand and looking through a nearby window, "You've quite a view from here."
Below them stood the old soot-eaten Gothic cathedral in a field of flat black gravestones. Beyond rose the hill of the Necropolis, its sides cut into by the porches of elaborate mausoleums, the summit prickly with monuments and obelisks. The topmost monument was a pillar carrying a large stone figure of John Knox, hatted, bearded, gowned and upholding in his right hand an open granite book. The trees between the tombs were leafless, for it was late autumn. Mrs. Thaw smiled and whispered wanly, "I saw a funeral go in there this morning." "No, it's not a very cheery outlook."

Mr. Thaw explained to his children that it would be weeks before their mother was well enough to come home and some months after that before she was able to leave her bed. The household would need to be reorganized, its duties distributed between the three of them. This reorganization was never effectively managed. Thaw and Ruth quarrelled too much about who should do what; moreover, Thaw was sometimes prevented by illness from working at all and Ruth thought this a trick to make her work harder and called him a lazy hypocrite. Eventually nearly all the housework was done by Mr. Thaw, who washed and ironed the clothes at the weekend, made breakfast in the morning and kept things vaguely tidy. Meanwhile, the surfaces of linoleum, furniture and windows became dirtier and dirtier.

At Whitehill School the pressure of work seemed to slacken for Thaw. The Higher Leaving Examination, the culmination of five years of schooling, was a few months away, and all around him his schoolmates crouched over desks and burrowed like moles into their studies. He watched them with the passionless regret with which he saw them play football or go to dances: the activity itself did not interest, but the power to share it would have made him less apart. The teachers had stopped attending to pupils who would certainly pass or certainly fail and were concentrating on the borderline cases, so he was allowed to study the subjects he liked (art, english, history) according to his pleasure, and in Latin or mathematics classes sat writing or sketching in a notebook as far from the teacher as possible. After Christmas he was told he would not be put forward for his leaving certificate in Latin, and this gave an extra six hours a week to use as he pleased. He used them for art. The art department was in whitewashed low-ceilinged rooms at the top of the building, and nowadays he spent most of his time there making an illuminated version of the Book of Jonah. Sometimes the art teacher, a friendly old man, looked over his shoulder to ask a question.

"Er . . . is this meant to be humorous, Duncan?"

"No sir."

"Why have you given him a bowler hat and umbrella?"

"What's humorous about bowler hats and umbrellas?"

"Nothing! I use an umbrella myself, in wet weather. . . . Do you mean to do anything special with this when you have completed it?"

Thaw meant to give it to Kate Caldwell. He mumbled, "I don't know."

"Well, I think you should make it less elaborate and finish it as soon as possible. No doubt it will impress the examiner, but he's more likely to be impressed by another still life or a drawing of a plaster cast."

Occasionally at playtime he went onto the balcony outside the art room and looked into the hall below where the captain of the football team, the school swimming champion and several prefects usually stood laughing and chatting with Kate Caldwell, who sat with a girlfriend on the edge of a table under the war memorial. Her laughter and hushed breathless voice floated up to him; he thought of going down and joining them, but his arrival would produce an expectant silence and revive the rumour that he loved her.

One day he came from the art room and saw her walk along the balcony on the other side of the hall. She smiled and waved and on an impulse he glared back timidly, opened the door behind him and beckoned. She came round, smiling with her mouth open. He said, "Would you like to see what I'm doing? In art, I mean?"

"Oh, that would be lovely, Duncan."

The only other student in the art room was a prefect called MacGregor Ross who was copying a sheet of Roman lettering. Thaw brought a folder of work from a locker and laid the pictures one after another on a desk in front of her.

"Christ arguing with the doctors in the temple," he said. "The mouth of Hell. This is a fantastic landscape. Mad flowers. These are illustrations I did for a debating society lecture. . . ."

She greeted each picture with small gasps of admiration and surprise. He showed her the unfinished Book of Jonah. She said, "That's wonderful, Duncan, but why have you given him a bowler hat and an umbrella?"

"Because he was that kind of man. Jonah is the only prophet who didn't want to be a prophet. God forced it on him. I see him as a fat middle-aged man with a job in an insurance office, someone naturally quiet and mediocre whom God has to goad into courage and greatness."

Kate nodded dubiously.

"I see. And what will you do with it when it's finished?"

Duncan's heart started thumping against his ribs. He said, "I'll mibby give it to you. If you'd like it."

She smiled flashingly and said, "Oh, thank you, Duncan, I'd love to have it. That's wonderful of you. It really is. . . . And what are *you* so busy with?" she asked, going over to MacGregor Ross. She pulled a stool up to MacGregor Ross's desk and spent twenty minutes with her head close beside his while he showed her how to use a lettering pen.

Mrs. Thaw left the Infirmary early in the new year. Mrs. Gilchrist downstairs and one or two other neighbours came into the house to prepare it for her, and dusted, washed and polished into the obscurest corner of every room.

"You'll have to be specially nice to your mother and help her all you can now," they said severely. "Remember, she won't be able to leave bed for a long time."

"Interfering old bitches," said Ruth.

"They mean well," said Thaw tolerantly. "They just have an unfortunate way of putting things."

Mrs. Thaw came home by ambulance and was tucked into the big bed in the front bedroom. She was allowed to sit by the fire in the evenings and soon gained enough strength for her children to quarrel with her without feeling very guilty. Thaw

brought home the completed "Book of Jonah." She took it
on her knee, looked thoughtfully through, asked him to explain
certain details then said seriously, "You know, Duncan, you
would make a good minister."

"A minister? Why a minister?"

"You have a minister's way of talking about things. What are
you going to do with this?"

"I'm giving it to Kate Caldwell."

"Kate Caldwell! Why? *Why?*"

"Because I love her."

"Don't be stupid, Duncan. What do you know about love?
And she certainly won't appreciate it. Ruth tells me she's nothing but a wee flirt."

"I'm not giving it to her because she'll appreciate it. I'm giving
it because I love her."

"That's stupid. Totally stupid. You'll have the whole school
laughing at you."

"The school's laughter is no concern of mine."

"Then you're a bigger fool than I thought. You've no sense
or pride or backbone at all and you'll marry and be made
miserable by the first silly girl who takes a fancy to ye."

"You're probably right."

"But I shouldn't be right! You ought not to let me be right!
Why can't you . . . oh, I give up. I give up. I give up."

The skin disease returned and his throat looked as if he
had made an incompetent effort to cut it. Each morning he
went to his mother's bedside and she wound a silk scarf tightly
round up to his chin and fixed it with small safety pins, giving
his head and shoulders a rigid look. One morning he entered
a classroom and found Kate Caldwell's eyes upon him. Perhaps
she had expected someone else to come in, or perhaps she
had looked to the door in a moment of unfocused reverie,
but her face took on a soft look of involuntary pity, and seeing
it he was filled by pure hatred. It stamped his face with an
implacable glare which stayed for a second after the emotion
faded. Kate looked puzzled, then turned with a toss of the
head to some gossiping friends. That night, without any sense
of elation, Thaw gave the "Book of Jonah" to Ruth and afterward sat glumly by his mother's bed.

"Do you know something, Duncan?" said Mrs. Thaw. "Ruth
will appreciate that a thousand times more than Kate Caldwell."

"I know. I know," he said. There was an ache between his
heart and stomach as if something had been removed.

"Ach, son, son," said Mrs. Thaw, holding out her arms to him, "never mind about Kate Caldwell. Ye've always your auld mither."

He laughed and embraced her saying, "Yes, mither, I know, but it's not the same thing, it's not the same thing at all."

The Higher Leaving Examination arrived and he sat it with no sense of special occasion. In the invigilated silence of the examination room he glanced through the mathematics paper and grinned, knowing he would fail. It would be too conspicuous to get up and walk out at once so he amused himself by trying to solve two or three problems using words instead of numbers and writing out the equations like dialectical arguments, but he was soon bored with this, and confronting the supervising teacher's raised and condemning eyebrows with an absentminded stare he handed in his papers and went upstairs to the art room. The other examinations were as easy as he had expected.

Mrs. Thaw had grown gradually stronger but at the time of the exams she caught a slight cold and this caused a setback. She only got up now to go to the lavatory. Mr. Thaw said, "Don't you think you should use the bedpan?"
She laughed and said, "When I can't go to the lavatory myself I'll know I'm done for."
One evening when Thaw was alone with her in the house she said, "Duncan, what's the living room like?"
"It's quite warm. There's a good fire on. It's not too untidy."
"I think I'll get up and sit by the fire for a bit."
She pulled the bedclothes back and put her legs down over the edge of the bed. Thaw was disturbed to see how thin they were. The thick woollen stockings he pulled on for her would not stay up but hung in folds round her ankles.
"Just like two sticks," she said, smiling. "I've turned into a Belsen horror."
"Don't be *daft!*" said Thaw. "There's nothing wrong that another month won't cure."
"I know, son, I know. It's a long, slow process."
At this time Thaw slept with his father in the bed settee. He did not sleep well, for the mattress had a hollow in the middle which Mr. Thaw, being heavier, naturally filled, and Thaw found it hard not to roll down on top of him. One night after the lights were out he remarked how pleasant it would be to get back to the usual sleeping arrangements when his

mother was better. After a pause, Mr. Thaw said strangely, "Duncan, I hope you're not . . . hoping too much that your mother will get better." Thaw said lightly, "Oh, where there's life there's hope."

"Duncan, there's no hope. You see, the operation was too late. She's been recovering from the effects of the operation, but it's a recovery that can't last. Her liver is too badly damaged."

Thaw said, "When will she die then?"

"In a month. Mibby in two months. It depends on the strength of her heart. You see, the liver isn't cleaning the blood, so her body is getting less and less nourishment."

"Does she know?"

"No. Not yet."

Thaw turned his face away and wept a little in the darkness. His tears were not particularly passionate, just a weak bleeding of water at the eyes.

He was wakened by a crash and a great cry. They found his mother struggling on the lobby floor. She had been trying to go to the lavatory. "Ach, Daddy, I'm done. I'm done. Finished," she said as Mr. Thaw helped her back to bed. Thaw stood transfixed at the living-room door, his brain ringing with echoes of the cry. At the moment of waking to it he had felt it was not an unexpected thing, but something heard ages ago which he had waited all his life to hear again.

Two days later Thaw and Ruth came home from school together and had the door opened to them by Mr. Thaw. He said, "Your mother has something to tell you."

They entered the bedroom. Mr. Thaw stood by the door watching. The bed had been moved to the window to give her a view of the street, and she lay with her face toward them and said timidly, "Ruth, Duncan, I think that one day soon I'll just . . . just sleep away and not wake up."

Ruth gasped and ran from the room and Mr. Thaw followed her. Thaw went to the bed and lay on it between his mother and the window. He felt below the covers for her hand and held it. After a while she said, "Duncan, do you think there's anything afterwards?"

He said, "No, I don't think so. It's just sleep."

Something wistful in the tone of the question made him add, "Mind you, many wiser folk than me have believed there's a new life afterwards. If there is, it won't be worse than this one."

For several days on returning from school he took his shoes off and lay beside his mother holding her hand. It would have been untrue to say he felt unhappy. At these times he hardly thought or felt at all, and did not talk, for Mrs. Thaw was becoming unable to talk. Usually he looked out at the street. Although joining a main road it was a quiet street and usually lit by cold spring sunshine. The houses opposite were semi-detached villas with lilacs and a yellow laburnum tree in the gardens. If he felt anything it was a quietness and closeness amounting to contentment. During this time Ruth, who had never taken much interest in household things, became very busy at cleaning and cooking and made her mother many light sorts of foods and pastries, but soon Mrs. Thaw had to be nourished on nothing but fluids and was too weak to speak clearly or open her eyes. Nobody in the household talked much, but once Thaw made a remark to his sister beginning. "When Mummy's dead . . ."

"She's not going to die."

"But Ruth . . ."

"She's not *going* to die. She's going to get better," said Ruth, staring at him brightly.

At school oral examinations were held to corroborate the results of the written exams. The English teacher told his students to learn by heart some passages of prose, preferably from the bible, since they might be asked to recite aloud. Thaw decided to shock the examiner by learning the erotic verses from the Song of Solomon which begin, "Behold thou art fair, my love, behold thou art very fair." On the morning of the English oral he went after breakfast to say cheerio to his mother. Mr. Thaw was sitting by the bed holding one of her hands between both of his. She lay back on the pillows, a line of white showing below her almost closed eyelids. She was mumbling desperately, "I aw ie, I aw ie."

"All right, all right, Mary," said Mr. Thaw. "You won't die. You won't die."

"Uh I *aw* ie, I *aw* ie."

"Don't worry, you're not going to die, you're not going to die."

For the first time in two weeks Mrs. Thaw shuddered and sat up. Her eyes opened to the full, she pulled her lips back from her teeth and shrieked, "I want to die! I want to die!" and fell back. Thaw collapsed on a chair, holding his head between his hands and sobbing loudly. Ten minutes later he ran to

school across the sunlit slope of the park, loudly chanting verses
from the Song of Solomon. When he got home that afternoon
Mrs. Thaw lay more quiet and still than ever and breathed
with a faint wheezy sound. He put his lips to her ear and
whispered urgently, "Mum! Mum! I've passed in English. I've
got Higher English."
A faint smile moved her mouth, then sank into her blind face
like water into sand. Next morning when Mrs. Gilchrist downstairs came in to wash her and pulled the curtain behind the
bed she heard a very faint whisper: "Another day," but in
the afternoon word that Thaw had passed in Art and History
did not reach the living part of her brain, or else she had
grown indifferent.

   She died three days later, very early on a Saturday morning.
The previous night Mrs. Gilchrist downstairs and Mrs. Wishaw
from across the landing sat waiting in the living room and
did not move out when Thaw went to bed there. Mr. Thaw
sat in the bedroom holding his wife's hand. When Thaw awoke
the light was filtering through the curtains and the neighbours
had left and he knew his mother was dead. He got up, dressed,
ate a bowl of cornflakes and switched the wireless on to a
comedy programme. Mr. Thaw came in and said, slightly embarrassed, "Would you mind turning it down a bit, Duncan?
The neighbours might be offended if they heard."
Thaw switched off the wireless and went for a walk to the
canal. He stood at the edge of a deep stone channel and watched
without thought or feeling the foam-flecked water swirl between
rotting timbers.

   In the afternoon he called on Coulter as he had arranged
to do some while before. Mrs. Coulter had taken her husband
for a walk, and Thaw sat by the fire while Coulter, in vest
and trousers, washed at the sink. Thaw said awkwardly, "By
the way, Bob, my mother died last night."
Coulter turned slowly round. He said "You're joking, Dun-
can."
"No."
"But I saw her two weeks ago. She was talking to me. She
seemed all right."
"Aye."
Coulter towelled his hands, looking at Thaw closely. He said,
"You shouldn't hold it in, Duncan. It'll be worse for you later."
"I don't think I'm holding anything in."

Coulter pulled a shirt and pullover on and said in a worried way, "The bother is, I arranged tae meet Sam Lang at Tollcross playing fields at three. We were going to do some running practice. I thought you wouldnae mind coming along."

"I don't mind coming along."

When he got home the undertaker had called. A coffin lay on a pair of trestles on the rug before the bedroom fireplace. The lid was placed to leave a square hole at the top and Mrs. Thaw's face stuck up through the hole. Thaw looked at it with puzzled distaste. The features had been his mother's but though he saw no difference in the shape all resemblance had vanished. The thing was without even the superficial life of a work of art and its material lacked the integrity of bronze or clay. He touched the brow with a fingertip and felt cold bone under the cold skin. This dense pack of dead tissues was not his mother's face. It was nobody's face.

In the days before the funeral the bedroom was pervaded by a sweet fusty odour which spread to other parts of the house. Air fresheners of the kind used in lavatories were placed under the coffin but made little difference. On Tuesday the minister of Mrs. Thaw's church conducted a short service in the living room while the coffin was screwed tight and taken deftly downstairs to the hearse. The living room was crowded with neighbours and old friends and relatives whom Thaw had heard his parents speak of but hardly ever met. Twice or thrice during the service the door was furtively opened and those beside it shifted to admit a stealthily breathing old man or woman. Thaw stood by the sideboard wearing his newest suit. It struck him that the minister had not visited his mother during the last weeks, and this not through failure of duty (he was a young earnest nervous man) but because his presence would have been an intrusion. To Mrs. Thaw and her friends the church had been a gathering place. They went to a service on Sunday, and on Thursday to a social club in the church hall, but none could have been accused of piety. Mrs. Thaw had been shocked when, some years before, Thaw called himself an atheist, but no more shocked than when, shortly afterward, he called himself a Christian and started turning the other cheek in his fights with Ruth. A phrase came into his head: "The consolations of religion." As far as he could see, his mother had lived and died without consolations of any kind at all.

The service ended and he went down to the cars with his father, the minister and a few others. The cars were shining black Rolls-Royces with silent engines and as they sped through the streets of the northern suburbs he looked out of the window feeling comfortable and privileged. It was a grey day, a lid of grey sky had shut down on Glasgow and thin smirr fell from it. They came to a municipal cemetery so precisely on the edge of the city that on three sides it was surrounded by open fields. There was a delay at the gate. The cars halted in a line behind the cars of a funeral party ahead. After a while the cars in front disappeared and they went up a curving drive between dripping rhododendrons and stopped outside a miniature Victorian-gothic church with a smokestack behind. More neighbours and relatives were waiting at the porch and followed Thaw and his father inside. They stood in the front row of pews and everyone else crowded into the pews behind. Just before them was a tall pulpit, and to the right of it a low platform with the coffin on top. Coffin and platform were covered by a heavy red cloth. After a moment of silence Thaw began to wonder why nobody sat down. The same thought must have struck his father, for he sat down and everyone followed his example. The minister, in the black gown and white bands of a doctor of divinity, climbed into the pulpit, said a prayer and announced a hymn. Everyone stood and sang and sat down again. The minister produced a sheet of paper and said, "Before we proceed with the service I have been asked—er, to read this to you:

"During the last few months of her illness Mary Thaw was completely confined to her bed. I would like to thank those many good friends and neighbours who made these months as pleasant for her as they could. They brought gifts of fruit and of cake, and the even more precious gift of their company. I would like to tell them on her behalf how very much she appreciated their attentions, and to extend to them the thanks that she herself is unable to extend today."

In the pews behind somebody sniffed and blew their nose. Thaw looked sideways at his father and whispered, "That was very good." The service continued. At the words "Dust to dust and ashes to ashes," there began a lumbering rumbling sound and the red cloth began to sag as the coffin was drawn down under it. For a second it bulged up again with a rush of air from below, then flopped so that a rectangular depression appeared where the coffin had been. Thaw was struck by a poignant sense of loss neutralized at once by a memory of a conjuror who had made a scone disappear from under a handkerchief.

Outside the church people squared their shoulders and began talking in loud cheerful voices.
"Well, that didn't go too badly, did it?"
"A beautiful service, beautiful."
"Hullo, hullo! There's a voice I've not heard in many a long day. How are ye, Jim?"
"No' too bad. A beautiful service, wasn't it?"
"Aye, beautiful. I liked that bit the minister read out in the middle."
"Ye cannae beat good neighbours."
"Aye, but she deserved good neighbours. She was one hersel'."
"Who's that waiting by the gate? Don't tell me it's auld Neil Bannerman?"
"Aye, it's Neil Bannerman."
"My God, he looks done. Really done. Fancy auld Neil Bannerman surviving Mary Thaw. Last time I saw him was at her father's funeral ten years back."
"Is it true, er, there's a quantity of refreshment, er, available somewhere?"
"Aye, man, there's a tea laid on at the Grand Hotel at Charing Cross. Come in my car."
The male relations gathered in a private room of a hotel in Sauchiehall Street and ate a high tea of cold ham and warm vegetables. They chattered about old acquaintances and football and the days when the local churches had their own football teams. Thaw sat silent among them. At one point Bernard Shaw was mentioned and he was asked to tell an anecdote about him. It was well received. Afterward he returned with his father in someone's car. The rain was falling heavily now. He thought how pleasant it would be to get home and sit by the bedroom fire drinking tea with his mother, then remembered this was impossible.

Mr. Thaw wanted his wife's ashes scattered on a hillside overlooking Loch Lomond where they had walked together in their courting days. One windy and sunny spring morning he journeyed with his children to Loch Lomond by train. Thaw held the oblong deal box with the ashes in it upon his knee.

The lid lacked hinge or fastening, and he raised it once or twice and looked curiously at the soft grey stuff inside. It was exactly like cigarette ash. Mr. Thaw said, "Be careful, Duncan." Duncan said, "Yes, we don't want to spill her before we get there."

He was surprised to see his father look shocked. They climbed the hillside by a stony lane sunk among bracken and budding hedges. Higher up this became a cart track over a green field, then they went through a gap in a dry-stone dyke and it became a sandy path among heather with curlews crying around it. Near the path lay a flat rock with a hole in the middle where the Colquhoun clan once stuck their banner pole when gathering to fight.

"I suppose this place is as good as any," said Mr. Thaw.

They sat and rested, looking down on the loch and the green islands in it. Northward the jagged wall of the highland bens looked distinct and solid enough to bang the knuckles against. They waited till a young couple who had paused to see the view passed out of sight, then opened the box and flung handfuls of ash into the air. The wind whisked it away like smoke into the heather.

A fortnight after Mr. Thaw sat at his desk in the living room and said, "Duncan, come here. I want ye to look at this. It's the bill for your mother's funeral. A fantastic figure, isn't it? You'd think cremation would be a lot cheaper than burial, but no. The costs are practically the same."

Thaw looked at the bill and said, "Aye, it does look a bit extravagant."

"Well, I'm not going to have that sum of money wasted on me, so I'm arranging to give my body to science. Would ye sign this paper? It's to prove that as next of kin you have no objection."

Thaw signed.

"Good. The arrangement is that when I die you inform the medical faculty of the university and they call and collect me with an iron coffin. If you do that within twenty-four hours, you and Ruth will be given ten pounds to divide between you, so you see it's not only cheaper, it's profitable."

"I'll spend the money drinking to the health of your memory," said Thaw.

"If you've sense you'll spend it otherwise."

Almost a year later Thaw was looking through a drawer when he found a letter in his mother's handwriting. It was written very faintly in pencil and was a rough draft of a letter she probably never got round to sending. It was superscribed to the correspondence page of a cheap woman's magazine.

> *I have enjoyed very much the letters from your readers telling about the funny mistakes some children make. I wonder if you would like to print an experience of mine. When my wee son was six or seven, we left the house one night quite late and were looking up at the stars. Suddenly Duncan said, "Where's the tractor?" His father had been teaching him the names of the stars, and he had got mixed up with the plough. I have not been very well recently and have had to spend most of the time in bed. I find my main pleasure nowadays in memories like these.*

Thaw stood awhile with the letter in his hand. He remembered the night she spoke of. It had been at the hostel in Kinlochrua at Christmas. The family had been going to a concert in the main building, and the question had been asked by Ruth. Mrs. Thaw had always preferred him to Ruth and had unconsciously transferred the incident. He put back the letter and shut the drawer. Grief pulled at an almost unconscious corner of his mind like a puppy trying to attract its master's attention by tugging the hem of his coat.

CHAPTER 20. Employers

The Higher Leaving Examination results were not yet published, but almost everyone knew how well or badly they had done and the school was full of excited discussions about maximum salaries and minimum qualifications. Employment officers came and lectured on careers in accountancy, banking and the civil service. A lawyer talked about law, an engineer about engineering, a doctor about medicine and a major about the army. A Scottish Canadian lectured on the advantages of emigration. Students argued in groups about whether it was best to stay a sixth year at school and win more certificates or leave at once for university or commercial or technical colleges. Mr. Thaw said, "So what are you going to do?"

"I don't know."

"What do you want to do?"

"That's irrelevant, isn't it?"

"Face facts, Duncan. If you can't live by doing what you want, you must take the nearest thing to it you can get."

"I want to write a modern Divine Comedy with illustrations in the style of William Blake."

"Well, surely the sensible thing to try for is work as a commercial artist?"

"For that I need four years at art school and you cannae afford to send me."

Mr. Thaw looked thoughtful. He said, "When I worked for Laird's, the box-makers, I was fairly friendly with Archie Tulloch, who was head of the art department. They used to take in boys of sixteen or seventeen then. They designed labels for packages and cartons, you know, and patterns for wrapping paper. That might not gratify your bohemian soul, but it would be a start. If I wrote to Archie Tulloch he would likely look your work over."

Thaw got an afternoon off school and walked down into Bridgeton wearing a newly cleaned overcoat and with a folder of work under his arm. The factory was near the river and he descended to it by narrow streets where many small factories stood between tenements and scrapyards. The sky was grey and beyond the rooftops the Cathkin Braes looked flat and dark like a wall shutting the city in, though he could make out the silhouettes of trees on the skyline. He remembered his mother talking about these trees when he was very small. They had reminded her of a line of camels in the desert. The ceiling of cloud pressed lower and released a thin smirr like a falling mist. It glazed the streets until they reflected the pale sky, a seagull skimming above the street appeared as far below it. The city seemed hung among distances of grey air, and windows were raised from the bottom and hands placed potted ferns on the sills to be watered. The rain soothed Thaw's misery. He started to feel confident, and to imagine coming often this way to Laird's. Even when very rich he would walk through these streets with such regularity that folk who lived there would set their clocks by him. He would be part of their lives. He came to a factory which was a huge brick cube at the junction of two streets. He straightened his tie, ran a hand through his hair, gripped the folder tightly and pushed through a revolving door of brass, glass and carved mahogany.

The entrance hall was a bare place with a small door marked INQUIRIES. He turned the knob and entered a wedge-shaped room with a switchboard and an elderly lady shut in a corner by a counter of polished yellow wood. The lady said, "Yes?"
"I've an appointment; that's to say I'm expected. Mr. Tulloch expects me."
"What is your name, please?"
He said shyly, "I am Duncan Thaw."
The lady moved her fingers among clicking plugs and said, "Mr. Tulloch? A Mr. Thaw to see you. He says he has an appointment. . . . Very well."
She deftly fingered more switches.
"Would you send down a junior? To take a Mr. Thaw to the waiting room? . . . Very well. . . . Would you wait here a little while, sir?"
"Yes, please," said Thaw, humbled at being called sir. He went to a low table with magazines arranged neatly on top in overlapping rows. Lacking the courage to disturb their order, he was content to look at the covers:

The Executive—A MAGAZINE FOR THE MODERN BUSINESSMAN.

Modern Business—A MAGAZINE FOR THE EXECUTIVE.

Ingot—THE THUNDERHAUGH STEEL GROUP MONTHLY BULLETIN.

Automobile—THE CAR DEALERS' MONTHLY BULLETIN.

They had the thin glossy covers of obscene novelettes and were mostly pictures of people in expensive clothes sitting behind desks.

A small neat pretty girl came in and said, "Mr. Thaw? Will you come this way, please?"
He walked behind her across the bare hall and climbed some wide metallic stairs. She hurried ahead of him through corridors of glass and cream-coloured metal, smiling downward as if sharing a tender secret with her bosom, and left him at a door labelled WAITING ROOM. Inside four men sat round a table, one of them saying in an English Midland dialect, "Yes, but what I don't understand is—"
"Will you excuse us?" said another man swiftly to Thaw. Thaw sat down in a comfortable chair and said, "Certainly. Please go on. I'm only here to wait."
"Then would you wait outside?" said the swift man, rising and opening the door. Thaw sat feeling insulted on a sofa against the corridor wall. It occurred to him that the men inside were capitalists plotting something. This floor of the factory was cut up into offices by glass screens supported by metal walls. The glass was rippled so that only shadows could be seen through it, and the bleakness, coldness, metallicness of the place gave a resounding quality to footsteps, clattering typewriters, ringing telephones, and the mutter of administrative voices. Two long spectacled men paused at a corner.
"I think I'd better check that teller."
"No no. No need for that at all."
"Still, if the figures aren't exact—"
"No no. Even if his figures are a hundred percent out, that's enough for my purpose."

Thaw realized Mr. Tulloch was beside him. He was a weary, paunchy man who said, "Duncan Thaw? . . . Yes . . ." and sat down.

"I haven't much time. Show me your stuff."

Thaw suddenly felt competent and businesslike. He opened his folder and said "Here is a series of watercolours, a series dealing with acts of God. The Deluge. The Tower of Babel. The Walls of Jericho Falling Flat."

"Um. Mmm. Next?"

"Penelope unweaving. Circe. Scylla and Charybdis. The last is least successful because at the time I was equally influenced by Blake and Beardsley and the two sorts of outline—"

"Yes. And this?"

"The Cave Artist. Moses on Sinai. Greek Civilization. Roman Imperialism. The Sermon on the Mount. Vandals. The Cathedral City. John Knox preaching to Mary Queen of Scots. The Factory City. The—"

Mr. Tulloch suddenly sat back and Thaw grinned at the air before him and shuffled the pictures back into the half-emptied folder. Mr. Tulloch was saying, ". . . take them at intervals of five years, so you see we really have no room for you. Your work, however, is very promising. Yes. Perhaps something in the illustrative line. Have you tried McLellan the publisher?"

"Yes, but—"

"Oh, yes, ha, ha, well of course the business is overcrowded just now. . . . Have you tried Blockcrafts, Bath Street? Well, try them. Ask for Mr. Grant and say I sent you. . . ." They stood up together. "Apart from that, you see, there's nothing I can do."

"Yes," said Thaw. "Thankyou very much."

He smiled and wondered if the smile looked bitter. It felt bitter. Mr. Tulloch conducted him to the head of the staircase and gave him a tired smile and an unexpectedly firm handshake. "Goodbye. I'm sorry," he said.

Thaw hurried into the drab street, feeling cheapened and defeated. He remembered with an odd pang that Mr. Tulloch had not once asked about his father.

A week later Thaw and his father saw the headmaster of Whitehill School, a white-moustached man who regarded them kindly from behind his desk. He said "Duncan, Mr. Thaw, has very strong imaginative powers. And undoubted talent. And his own way of seeing things, unfortunately." He smiled. "I say unfortunately because this makes it hard for plodding mediocrities like you and me to help him. You agree?"

Mr. Thaw laughed and said, "Oh, I agree all right. However, we must do our best."

"However, we must do our best. Now I think Duncan would be happiest in some job without too much responsibility, a job that would leave him plenty of spare time to develop his talents as he pleases. I see him as a librarian. He's good with books. I see him as a librarian in some small highland town like Oban or Fort William. What do you think, Mr. Thaw?"

"I think, Mr. McEwan, it is a very satisfactory *idea*. But is it a *possibility?*"

"I think so. To enter the library service two higher and two lower certificates are required. Duncan's higher art and english and lower history are guaranteed.The maths results aren't out yet. How do you think he did?"

Mr. Thaw said, "Well, Duncan?"

As the firm responsible voices passed his future gravely backward and forward between them Thaw sank into a fatalistic doze. It took him a moment to notice he was expected to speak. He said, "I've failed in maths."

"Why are you sure?"

"To pass I need full marks for everything I wrote, and what I wrote was mostly nonsense."

"Why does someone of your intelligence write nonsense after four years of study?"

"Laziness, I suppose."

The headmaster raised his eyebrows. "Indeed? The problem is, would you continue to be so lazy if your father was prepared to allow you another year at school?"

Mr. Thaw said, "In other words, Duncan, will you study for a certificate in lower maths if Mr. McEwan allows you another year at school?"

As Thaw considered this a grin began upon his face. He tried to suppress it and failed. The headmaster smiled and said to Mr. Thaw, "He's thinking of all the reading and painting he'll be able to do with practically no supervision at all. Is that not so, Duncan?"

Thaw said, "And mibby I'll be able to go to evening classes at the art school."

The headmaster struck the desk with his hand and leaned over it. "Yes!" he said seriously. "A year of freedom! But it has to be bought. The price is not high, but are you prepared to pay it? Do you faithfully promise your father to study and master your trigonometry and algebra and geometry? Do you promise to attend your mathematic lessons, not only in body but in spirit?"

Thaw hung his head and muttered, "Yes, sir."

"Good, good. Mr. Thaw, I think you have an assurance you can depend upon."

Next day Thaw met the mathematics teacher as he crossed the hall. She looked at him brightly and said, "What happened to you, Thaw?"

He was puzzled. She smiled and said, "Haven't you been going around telling people you'd failed in maths?"

"Yes, Miss."

"Well, the official results have just been published. You've passed. Congratulations."

Thaw stared at her in horror.

Later that week he walked into the white marble entrance of the Mitchell Library. He had often come to this place to see facsimiles of Blake's prophetic books, and as a plump man in a brass-buttoned coat led him upstairs the air of scholastic calm and polite attention produced a lightening of the spirit. It might not be a bad thing to work in this place. He was conducted to a door at the end of a corridor with chequered marble floor and low white vaulted ceiling. The room within was thickly carpeted, with a vase of flowers on the marble mantelpiece and another on a desk at the window. A small old man behind the desk was reading a document. He said in a clogged voice, "Mr. Thaw? Pleaze take a zeat. I'll be able to attend to you in a minute."

Thaw sat uneasily. The man had a hole in the right side of his face where the cheek should have been and most of the face was twisted toward it. His right eye had been pulled out of line with the left and the eyeball was so exposed that when he blinked, which was often, the eyelid could not cover it. He laid the document down and said, "Zo you want to become a librarian."

The muscles working his tongue moved awkwardly and beads of saliva kept bouncing from it onto the desk. Thaw watched them in fascination, nodding and making quiescent sounds when these seemed appropriate.

". . . . . hourz nezezzarily ztaggered. You will work two eveningz per week till half pazt eight, but theze will be compen-

zated for by morningz off. You will be eczpected to attend
night glazzez on two other eveningz."

"To learn what?" said Thaw, with effort.

"Bookkeeping and cataloguing. There are zeveral zyztems of
cataloguing, each a world in itzelf. Each year you will zit an
eczamination and be promoted accordingly, and within five
yearz you zhould qualify for a zertificate qualifying you to aczept
the pozt of zenior librarian anywhere in the United Kingdom."

"Oh. Oh, good," said Thaw feebly.

"Yez, it *iz* good. *Very* good. But I'm afraid you can't ztart
for another zicz weeks. Only the head librarian can employ
you and he's viziting the You Ezz Ay juzt now. But he'll be
back in zicz weekz, and you'll zertainly be able to ztart then."

As Thaw left the building a change came upon him. It
was as if several pounds had been added to his weight, and
his heart had begun beating more sluggishly, and the air had
thickened in his lungs. His thoughts also became heavy and
thick. At home over tea he told his father about the interview.
Mr. Thaw sighed with relief.

"Thank God for that!" he said.

"Yes. Yes, thank *God*. Thank *God*. Yes, indeed, let us give
thanks to *God*."

"Duncan, what's wrong? What's the matter?"

"Nothing. Nothing. Things are as finely arranged as they can
be in a world of this sort. Praise be to the Maker and Upholder
of all things. Yes! Yes! Yes! Yes! Yes! Yes! Ye—"

"Stop! You're talking like a madman! If you won't state the
matter honestly then keep your mouth shut!"

Duncan shut his mouth. After a few minutes Mr. Thaw said
on a note of pleading, "Tell me the matter, Duncan."

"I had a wish to be an artist. Was that not mad of me? I had
this work of art I wanted to make, don't ask me what it was,
I don't know; something epic, mibby, with the variety of facts
and the clarity of fancies and all of it seen in pictures with a
queer morbid intense colour of their own, mibby a gigantic
mural or illustrated book or even a film. I didn't know *what*
it would have been, but I knew how to get ready to make it.
I had to read poetry and hear music and study philosophy and
write and draw and paint. I had to learn how things and people
felt and were made and behaved and how the human body
worked and its appearance and proportions in different situa-
tions. In fact, I had to eat the bloody moon!"

"Duncan, remember what your headmaster said! In four years

you can be head librarian in some small country town and *then* you can make yourself an artist. Surely a *real* artist could wait four years?"

"I don't know if he could. I know that none ever did. People in Scotland have a queer idea of the arts. They think you can be an artist in your *spare* time, though nobody expects you to be a spare-time dustman, engineer, lawyer or brain surgeon. As for this library in a quiet country place, it sounds hellishly like Heaven, or a thousand pounds in the bank, or a cottage with roses round the door, or the other imaginary carrots that human donkeys are shown to entice them into all kinds of nasty muck."

Mr. Thaw rested his elbows on the table and held his head in his hands. After a while he said, "Duncan, what do you want me to do? I want to help you. I'm your father, even though you've been haranguing me as if I was a social system. If I was a millionaire I'd gladly support ye in idleness while you developed your talents, but I'm a costing and bonus clerk, and fifty-seven years old, and my duty is to make you self-supporting. Show me an alternative to the library service and I'll help you toward it."

Tears slid down Thaw's immobile face. He said harshly, "I can't. There's no alternative. I have no choice but to cooperate with my damnation."

"Stop being melodramatic."

"Am I melodramatic? I'm saying what I believe as succinctly as I can."

They finished the meal in silence. Then Mr. Thaw said, "Duncan, go to the art school tonight. Join the evening classes."

"Why?"

"You've six weeks before you start work for the libraries. Use them for what you like doing most."

"I see. Get a taste of that life before I give it up for good. No thanks."

"Duncan, join the evening classes."

"No thanks."

That evening he waited in a corridor of the art school outside the registrar's office in a queue of other applicants. When his turn came he entered a spacious room and started walking toward a desk at the far end, conscious of pictorial and statuesque objects on either side. The man at the desk looked up as he approached. He had a large, spectacled face and a wide mouth with amused corners. He spoke drawlingly, with an expensive English dialect. "Good evening. What can I do for you?"

Thaw sat down and pushed onto the desk a filled in application form. The registrar looked at it and said, "I see you want to go to life classes, ah, Thaw. How old are you?"

"Seventeen."

"Still at school?"

"I've just left it."

"I'm afraid you're rather young for life drawing. You'll have to convince us that your studies are sufficiently advanced to fit you for it."

"I've some work here."

Thaw pushed his folder onto the desk. The registrar looked through it examining each picture carefully. He said, "Are the mounted ones part of a series?"

"They illustrate a lecture I once gave."

The registrar put a few pictures aside and looked at them again. He said, "Don't you think you should join us as a day student?"

"My father can't afford it."

"We could arrange a grant from the Corporation, you know. What are you intending to do?"

"Join the library service."

"Do you like the idea?"

"It seems the only thing possible."

"Honestly, I think you would be wasted in the library service. This is remarkable work. Quite remarkable. I take it you would *prefer* to come to the art school as a full-time day student?"

"Yes."

"Your address is on this form, of course. . . . What school did you go to?"

"Whitehill Senior Secondary."

"Have you a telephone?"

"No."

"Has your father's place of work a telephone?"

"Yes. Garngash nine-three-one-three."

"Well, Thaw, I'll be seeing you again. I'll keep this work if I may. I want to show it to the director."

Thaw shut the door behind him. He had entered the building in an exhausted mood and had maintained through the interview a colourless, almost listless manner. Now he eyed the corridor outside with an excited speculation. It was lined with salt-white casts of renaissance nobility and nude and broken gods and goddesses. A door among these opened and a hectic

little group of girls marched out and surrounded him for a
moment with swinging skirts and hair, scent, chatter, thighs
in coloured slacks and the sweet alien abundances of breasts.
". . . . . charcoal charcoal charcoal always charcoal. . . . ."
". . . Did you see the way he posed the model? . . ."
". . . . . Wee Davie gives me the horrors. . . ."
He ran down a staircase, through the entrance hall and into
the street. Too elated to wait for the tram he walked home
by a route which took in Sauchiehall Street, Cathedral Square
and the canal bank. He saw himself at the school of art, a
respected artist among artists: prominent, admired, desired. He
entered corridors of glamorous girls who fell silent, gazing at
him and whispering together behind their hands. He pretended
not to notice but if his look fell upon one she blushed or turned
pale. He soared into dreams of elaborate adventure all dimly
associated with art but culminating in a fancy that culminated
all his daydreams. There was a great hall lit by chandeliers
and floored with marble and with a vast staircase at the end
rising into the dark of a starless sky. On each side of the hall
stood all the women he had loved or who had loved him, all
the men they had loved and married, everyone superbly evil,
virtuous, wise, famous and beautiful and all magnificently
dressed. Then he himself, alone and in ordinary clothes, walked
down the centre of the hall and started unhurriedly climbing
the staircase toward some huge and ultimate menace at the
top. This menace overhung all humanity but only he was fit
to encounter it, although it was an encounter from which he
would not return. He climbed to a tragic crescendo in which
organs, solo voices and orchestras blended in a lament which
combined the most impressive effects of Beethoven, Berlioz,
Wagner and Puccini.

He got home after dark. Mr. Thaw said, "What kept you?"
"I walked back."
"Did they let you join the life class?"
"I'm not sure. The registrar asked me a lot of questions. He
thought I should join the day school. I told him it was impossi-
ble. He asked for your office telephone number."
Thaw spoke expressionlessly. Mr. Thaw said, "Well, well."
They ate supper in silence.

Mr. Thaw came home next day slightly earlier than usual
and slightly breathless. He sat facing Thaw across the living-
room hearth rug and said, "He phoned me this morning—

Peel, the registrar, I mean. He asked me if I could call and
see him. I'd been talking over this business with Joe McVean,
and Joe said, 'Duncan, you take the afternoon off. I'll manage
fine here myself.' So I went and saw Peel there and then.''

Mr. Thaw brought out his pipe and pouch and began filling
one from the other.

"You seem to have made an impression on that man. He said
your work was unusually good. He said it was rare for the
art school authorities to *persuade* someone to join. It had only
happened once in the last ten years. He said the director agreed
with him that you would be wasted as a librarian, and that
you could get a grant from the Corporation of a hundred and
fifty pounds a year. I said to him, 'Mr. Peel, I know nothing
about art. I do not appreciate my son's work. However, I can
vouch for his sincerity, and I accept your opinion as an expert
when you vouch for his ability. But tell me one thing: what
prospects has he when he finishes this four-year course of yours?'
"Well, he hummed and hawed a bit at that, then told me that
for someone of your talent there might well be a chance of
teaching in the art school when you had qualified. 'However,'
he said, 'the boy will be unhappy anywhere else, Mr. Thaw.
Let him decide himself what to do when the four years are
up. Don't rush him into a job he'll hate at this stage.' I said
I would think it over and tell him tomorrow. I went straight
from the art school to Whitehill and saw your headmaster.
Do you know what I found? Peel had phoned him and had a
talk with him. McEwan said to me, 'Mr. Thaw, that man is
better equipped to decide Duncan's future than you or I.' So
I phoned the art school and said you could join.''

"Thanks,'' said Thaw, and left the room. A minute later Mr.
Thaw came to him in the front bedroom, kneeling by the bed
with his face pushed into the coverlet. Indrawn moans came
from his muffled face and his back shuddered spasmodically.
Mr. Thaw said in a puzzled voice, "What's wrong, Duncan?
Don't you want to go to the art school? Aren't you glad?''

"Yes. Very glad.''

"Then why are ye greeting?''

Thaw stood up and dried his face with a handkerchief.

"I don't know. Relief, mibby.''

Mr. Thaw patted his son affectionately under the chin with
his clenched fist. "Cheer up!'' he said. "And if you don't make
another Picasso of yourself, I'll—I'll—I'll knock your block
off so I will.''

One hot afternoon Thaw and Coulter came down a wood-land path veined by tree roots and freckled with sunlight. Birds called in the green shadows above them. Coulter was talking about work. "At first the novelty made it not too bad. It was different from school, and you were getting paid, and you felt a *man;* you know, getting up and intae your clothes at seven, pulling at the day's first fag while your mother fried your break-fast, then down the road to the tram with your wee packet of sandwiches and sitting in your overalls with the other work-ers, crowding in at the gate and clocking on and then intae the machine shop—'Hullo,' 'Hullo, here it goes again,' 'You're fuckin' right it does'—and then the thumping and banging and feeling of danger—"

"Danger?" said Thaw.

"There's a bit of danger. You'll be battering away at something when the folk nearby start shouting. You wonder who they're yelling at this time, and they yell louder and it strikes you, 'Christ, what if it's me?' and you turn and there's a ten-ton girder swinging toward you on the overhead crane."

"That's hellish! Are there no rules against that sort of thing?"

"There's meant tae be a lane kept clear up the middle of the shed, but in a work like McHargs it's not easy."

Coulter chuckled.

"A weird thing happened the other day. This bloke was direct-ing the lowering of a girder from the crane; you know, he was standing underneath directing the lowering with his hands (you cannae hear a word in that din); you know—lower, lower, a bit to the left; all right, let it go now. The funny thing was, he was looking up at the bloke at the controls most of the time and he didnae notice that at the last moment he directed the girder to be lowered ontae his foot. He gave a scream like a soprano hitting a top note. We all looked to see what the matter was, but it took a while tae find out. He was standing up like the rest of us, only his foot was crushed under this girder. He couldnae even fall down!"

Thaw gave an appalled laugh and said, "You know that's very funny but—"

"Aye. Well, anyway, this business of being a *man* keeps you happy for mibby a week, then on your second Monday it hits you. To be honest the thought's been growing on you all through Sunday, but it really hits you on Monday: I've tae go on doing this, getting up at this hour, sitting in this tram in these overalls dragging on this fag, clocking on in this queue at the gate. 'Hullo, here we go again!' 'You're fuckin' right

we go!' and back intae the machine shop. You realize you'll
be spending more of your life in this place than anywhere,
excepting mibby bed. It's worse than school. School was compulsory—you were just a boy, you neednae take it seriously,
you could miss a day if your mammy was agreeable and wrote
a note. But engineering isnae compulsory. I chose it. And I'm
a man now. I have tae take it seriously, I *have* tae keep shoving
my face against this grindstone."
Coulter was silent for a while.
"Mind you, this feeling doesnae last. You stop thinking. Life
becomes a habit. You get up, dress, eat, go tae work, clock
in etcetera etcetera automatically, and think about nothing but
the pay packet on Friday and the booze-up last Saturday. Life's
easy when you're a robot. Then accidents happen that start
you *thinking* again. You know the Royal visit last week?"
"Aye."
"Well, there's a railway line at the back of the works, and
the Royal train was to go along it at three in the afternoon,
so the whole work got time off tae see it. So when the train
comes along there are four or five hundred of us at the edge
of the line in our greasy overalls. The Queen's in the first
carriage looking dead cool and gracious and waving; and in
the middle are a lot of old men like Lord Provosts with chains
round their necks, all waving like mad; and in a sort of observa-
tion car at the end sits the Duke in his wee yachting cap. He's
sitting at a table with a glass of something on it, and he gives
us a wave, but more offhand. And we all just stand there,
glowering."
Thaw laughed. "Did nobody wave? I think I'd have waved.
Just out of politeness."
"With the whole Union there? They'd have hanged ye. You
can laugh, Duncan, but the sight of the Duke set me back a
good three weeks. I havenae recovered from it yet. Why should
he be enjoying a dram in a comfortable train while I . . .
ach!" said Coulter disgustedly. "It's enough to make you rob
a bank. I've thought a lot about bank robbery recently. If I'd
even a remote chance of succeeding I'd try it too. I've no
faith in football pools."
Thaw said, "You're an apprentice. You won't be in the machine
shop for good."
"No. Six months in the machine shop, six months in the drawing
office, two nights a week at the technical college, and if I pass
the exams I'll be a qualified engineering draughtsman in three
years."

"And then things won't be too bad."

"Won't they? How did you feel about becoming a librarian?"

They crossed a stream by a plank bridge and came to an acre or two of level turf with a white flagpole in the middle. Lovers and picnic parties sat in the shade at the edge of the wood and children charged about playing anarchic ball games. A few benches on the other side of this green space overlooked the sky and had one or two elderly couples on them. Thaw and Coulter crossed to the benches and sat on one. They were on the edge of a plateau near the top of the Cathkin Braes, and a small rocky cliff went down from their feet to another level space noisy with child play and fringed by trees. From there the land sank in steep wooded terraces to a valley floor carpeted with rooftops and prickly with factory chimneys. To the east the Clyde could be seen meandering among farms, fields, pitheads and slag-bings, then Glasgow hid it till the course was marked by a skeletal procession of cranes marching into the west. Behind the city stood the long northern ridge of the Campsie Fells, bare and heather-green and creased by watercourses, and at this height they could see the Highland bens beyond them like a line of broken teeth. Everything looked unusually distinct, for it was Fair fortnight when big foundries stopped production and the smoke was allowed to clear.

"D'ye see Riddrie?" asked Thaw. "That reddish patch? Look, there's my old primary school on one side and Alexandra Park on the other. Where's your house?"

"Garngad's too low to be seen from here. I'm trying to see McHargs. It should be near those cranes behind Ibrox. Aye, there! There! The top of the machine shop is showing above those tenements."

"I should be able to see the art school, it's on top of a hill behind Sauchiehall Street—Glasgow seems all built on hills. Why don't we notice them when we're in it?"

"Because none of the main roads touch them. The main roads run east and west and the hills are all between."

On the grass at the foot of the cliff a big strong-bodied girl of about fourteen stood with legs apart and hands on hips between two piles of jackets. She wore a blue dress and grumbled impatiently as her younger brothers placed a football some distance in front of her and prepared to kick it at the goal mouth. Thaw stared at her in admiration. He said, "She's great. I'd like to draw her."

"Nude?"

"Anyhow."

"She's not exactly an oil painting. She's no Kate Caldwell."

"Damn Kate Caldwell."

They got up and walked on.

"Yes," said Coulter glumly. "You know what you want and you're in a place where they'll help you get it."

"It was an accident," said Thaw defensively. "If the head librarian hadnae been in America, and my Dad hadnae insisted I go to night classes, and the registrar hadnae been English and liked my work—"

"Aye, but it was an accident that *could* happen to you. Not to me. No accident but an atom bomb can get me out of engineering. I've no ambitions, Duncan. I'm like the man in Hemingway's story, I don't want to be special, I just want to feel good. And I'm in work that's only bearable if I feel as little as I can."

"In four months you'll be in the drawing office and learning something creative."

"Creative? What's creative about designing casings for machine units? I'll be better off, but because it's better wearing a clean suit than dirty overalls. And I'll get more money. But I won't *feel* good."

"It'll be years before I earn money."

"Mibby. But ye'll be doing what you want."

"True," said Thaw. "I'll be doing what I want. I suppose"—he turned and waved toward the city—"I'm nearly the luckiest man living here."

They re-entered the wood and came to a clearing with the iron structure of a child's swing in it. Thaw ran and jumped onto the wooden seat, grabbed the chains on each side and swung violently backward and forward in greater and greater arcs.

"Yah—yip—yeaaaaaaaaaaah!" he shouted. "I'll be doing what I want, won't I?"

Coulter leaned against the trunk of a tree and watched with a slight ironical grin.

INTERLUDE

The swing with Thaw on it flew high and stopped, leaving him in an absurd position with his knees higher than his back-flung head. The tree no longer rustled. Each branch and leaf was locked photographically in a single moment and as in old photographs the colour faded out, leaving the scene mono-chrome and brownish. Lanark stared at it through the ward window and said thoughtfully, "Thaw was not good at being happy."

The oracle said He was bad at it.

"Yet that is almost a happy ending."

A story can always end happily by stopping at a cheerful mo-ment. Of course in nature the only end is death, but death hardly ever happens when people are at their best. That is why we like tragedies. They show men ending energetically with their wits about them and deserving to do it.

"Did Thaw die tragically?"

No. He botched his end. It set no example, not even a bad one. He was unacceptable to the infinite bright blankness, the clarity without edge which only selfishness fears. It flung him back into a second-class railway carriage, creating you.

Lanark spread cheese on a slice of rye bread and said, "I don't understand that."

Rima's head stirred among the waves of blond hair on the pillow. Without opening her eyes she murmured, "Go on with the story."